# DANGER:
# FALLING
# ROCKS

A Dan Courtwright Mystery

*by*
PAUL WAGNER

This is a work of fiction. Names, characters, businesses, places, events, locales, and incidents are either the products of the author's imagination or used in a fictitious manner. Any resemblance to actual persons, living or dead, or actual events is purely coincidental.

Graphic Design by Mehdi Anvarian

Published by
Val de Grace Books, Inc.
Napa, California
valdegracebooks.com
(707) 259-5350

ISBN 978-0-9848849-6-4

First Edition

*For Estelle, who was far from home*
*and needed something to read.*

# chapter 1

Dan heard the bear before he saw it: a rough scratching, tearing noise that he mistook, just for an instant, for static on his radio. But it wasn't static; it was lower and rougher. It was a bear. And his radio wasn't on. He remembered that now and reached down very slowly to turn it back on. Maybe he was close enough to get some reception.

There was no mistaking the noise now, as the huge claws dug deeply into the tree bark. And then the noise changed to something even deeper as a layer of bark peeled off the tree with a hollow croaking sound.

It was coming from somewhere behind him on his left. He slowly turned his head and saw the bear, some seventy-five feet away, standing upright and tearing at a dead tree. A good-sized black bear, maybe two hundred and fifty pounds. The bear was focused on the potential for food in the tree, and didn't see Dan. Dan was captivated by the intimacy of the moment. The forest was still, with bright sunlight streaming through the trees; a few flies buzzed in the air. Dan found himself carefully breathing through his open mouth as he watched. The bear pursued its lunch, clawing at the bark of the tree, stopping to look for grubs and bugs, tasting with its tongue. Dan could see the delicate tongue reaching out, curling into the tree bark, then slipping quickly back inside its mouth. And out again. A huge paw delicately flicked at something in the bark; then the tongue slipped out again.

And then Dan's radio did crackle. A call for assistance up by Sonora Pass—a bad accident. Dispatch was asking for all units in the area to respond.

But that was not Dan's problem today. He turned it down quickly, but not quickly enough. At the end of five days in the backcountry, he was still far enough away from highways and accidents that he wasn't expected to answer the radio. As a ranger in the Emigrant Wilderness for the past four years, Dan Courtwright had learned when to listen to his radio, and when to shut it off.

The bear paused, trying to place the sound. He looked around and suddenly spotted Dan, frozen in place. The two of them watched each other for what seemed like a minute to Dan but was probably more like ten seconds. Sunlight from behind the bear made his fur seem to glow, as if he were wreathed in dandelion fluff, outlining his lean and powerful body and limbs. Moving first one paw, then another, the bear grudgingly wandered off behind the trees. Once he turned his head away from Dan, the bear didn't bother to look back. A tall, thin ranger with a trim beard clearly wasn't a threat.

Dan half-heartedly tried to follow at a discreet distance, trying to keep his footsteps silent, but soon lost the bear in the forested scrub. It was amazing how quickly and effectively an animal that large could disappear in the forest.

Out of curiosity, Dan walked over to try and find the tree that the bear had been scratching. There were quite a few in the little burned section of the forest, and three or four showed evidence of the bear.

"Not much food here today," thought Dan. He took another look around for the bear but could not even see tracks in the tough decomposed granite on the ground. From the direction the bear took, Dan doubted that he would run into the bear on the trail back to the lake, which was both a disappointment and a relief. Seeing a bear first and watching him was one thing; surprising a bear on the trail wasn't always so much fun.

He put down his pack on a low, flat slab of granite and pulled out his water bottle. Most of the new staff were big fans of bladders and hoses, but Dan still liked to carry his water in a bottle, and drink from the bottle rather than sucking from a tube. The water was still very cold from the stream earlier this morning, when Dan had pumped it full before he left camp.

The sun was now reaching that point in the morning where it was more than just light; it was also heat. And the contrast between the warmth of the sun on his back and the icy water going down his throat made Dan smile. It was a great morning in the mountains. He allowed his glance to slowly pan from tree to tree, with the deep blue sky behind. A woodpecker sounded off in the distance, too far for Dan to pick out in the forest.

After a few minutes' rest, Dan stood up and hefted his pack off the granite, swinging it easily onto one shoulder. Once he got his other arm through, he gave a little hop and lifted his shoulders to adjust his pack. The pack, now empty of all but a few energy bars and his gear, was wonderfully light. It always struck him as a pity that the best day to carry the pack was the last one. It made you want to turn around and go back up the trail, knowing that it would be easier now.

Still, he had plenty of time to cover the last six miles to the trailhead. He planned on stopping at Monument Lake to see how things were going with that big group there, just to see if they really had arrived, and to make sure they weren't making too much of a mess. Large groups sometimes got out of hand, and Dan wasn't afraid to make sure that they knew what was expected of them.

Besides, Kristen Gallagher was probably working as the cook there, and Dan liked the idea of stopping in to see her. He could tell her about the bear. She would like that. He liked the idea of making her smile. And maybe, if it looked like their schedules would work, he could ask her out to dinner on her day off. If he got the opportunity, and it wasn't too awkward.

Dan checked his watch. At this rate he'd get there a little early, but he could walk around the lake for a bit, and then maybe stay until lunch. That would still leave him a short four miles to the trailhead after lunch. And Kristen would have something better than energy bars to eat.

Perfect.

He gave one more glance to see if he could spot the bear again and headed off down the trail.

There are few things in life that are more alluring than the sight of a sparkling blue mountain lake seen through the trees as you walk down the trail. Dan could see occasional flashes of Monument Lake as he worked his way down the switchbacks of the trail hanging over the western ridge above the lake. But this was a trail that took most of his attention: rocky, crumbly, with enough big downward steps to keep his eyes more on the ground than on the scenery. A six-inch step is easy. An eight-inch step is still fine. But when they get to be a foot or more, it takes concentration with each footfall.

Dan always found trails like this to be slightly disappointing. They required so much attention to every footstep that it was hard to look around and enjoy the views that appeared and disappeared with every few feet of travel. And no two steps were alike. At least today, Dan had the consolation that his pack was lighter. He knew all too well how much pain a large step like this could create in his now-aging knees, particularly when the pack was full and heavy. Like all hikers, he would look for every advantage on a trail like this: a smaller rock that would allow him to reduce the size of the step, or even hiking along the stones on the edge of the trail, if they offered a path with smaller risers.

He had been on the trail long enough that his ankles had a few bruises where his other boot had smacked into them. And the very low, dull ache in his lower back let him know that it was time to take a day or two off. It was not just the hiking, but the bending over to do everything from putting on his socks to cooking his dinner. And his socks were already covered in dust from the trail, despite his having washed them out the night before.

The muscles in his legs were beginning to cramp from braking with every step, trying to keep him from falling down the steep trail. His knees ached, and he was grateful that the weight in the pack was as light as it was. With each step, his body weight seemed to thump into the ground. It was a relief to get down to the level of the lake, and the flatter section of the trail.

At the bottom of the trail was a huge granite boulder the size of a house, perched where it had fallen off the steep cliff somewhere above. The rock was massive, immeasurably heavy, with part of it buried deep in the earth. But somehow at some point it had crashed down the cliff. As he often did, Dan tried to imagine the scene when the boulder broke free of the cliff, bounced and thundered down the slope, and exploded to a shuddering stop. He tried to envision the ground trembling when it hit, imagining the forces involved. How big a cloud would it have made? And when did it fall? From the lichen and moss on the rock, Dan guessed it had fallen centuries ago, maybe much longer. But he also knew that the Sierra saw new rock falls every year—some of them as big as this one.

You could see that this was a place where hikers often stopped to rest. The ground was packed down around the trail junction, and the lone log had a slight polish to it where hundreds of hikers had sat and rested their sore shoulders and shaking knees. The branches on the top of the log were broken off, and a kind of trough was worn in the dirt in front of it. Dan passed it by, thinking that there would be better places to sit, and more interesting people to visit, at the camp ahead.

The next junction was with the trail around the lake, and it was just another hundred yards ahead. From that junction he might well see Kristen and the group camp at the foot of the lake. Once on the flat ground, his long stride allowed him to swing along easily, and he could feel the tight muscles of his thighs begin to loosen up now that they didn't have to keep him from plummeting down the staircase of the trail. That felt really good. He had to admit to that pleasure, even if it made him recognize the effects of his age on his body.

He saw the first tent, a small yellow bump in the trees, off to his left maybe two hundred yards past the junction, and was soon trying to count how many there were at the campsite. It was hard to tell without walking over for a full inspection, and Dan wasn't sure he was ready for that. There didn't appear to be anyone in camp—not Kristen or anyone else. Maybe it was too early for lunch, and Kristen was out on a hike or a swim.

He was disappointed but didn't really want to admit it. If he kept walking, the trail would take him quickly to the end of the lake, and then up over the notch to the steep two-mile downhill on the way to the trailhead. From there it was an easy two-mile stretch along the flat of the valley to the parking lot. He could probably do that in less than two hours, but that wouldn't get him to town in time for lunch. And there wasn't really a good spot to eat lunch on the dry trail between the lake and the trailhead.

Across the lake Dan could see the massive wall of the Monument, a name first given by rock climbers, and now officially recognized on the topo maps. It was a sheet of granite that rose in a wall some seven hundred feet above the lake. On the right the wall was fractured by a huge crack that ran from bottom to top like a deep black scar. In the middle of this scar were massive blocks of granite that were stacked high in the crevice. They stuck straight up above the lake along the face of the Monument like a tower of fat thumbs, hitching a ride. This was the route the climbers usually took to the top, negotiating through the crevices until they could reach a point high above the lake. At this point the crack began to slowly curve to the right, and the climbing got much easier.

But the left-hand side of the Monument was another story entirely. Polished to perfection by ancient glaciers, this face gave little hope for climbers, and only the very best even attempted it. The flawless chiseled granite gave few hand- or footholds, and no visible fissures. Endless years of erosion had left no marks on this face, only a few long streaks of black lichen to color the stone. The rest was a blank wall of stone, with subtle shades of grey and cream. The wall was unrelenting until you reached a small ledge about sixty feet from the top. From this ledge, the climb was easy, if you could forget about the five-hundred-foot free-fall that awaited you if you slipped.

Dan had climbed the right face, the Blockhead route, many years ago as a college student. He and a friend took almost all day to get to the top, and he vaguely remembered the tension of the climb and the exhilaration of their success. He smiled at the thought, knowing that he could not imagine tackling the route again.

The lake was ruffled with wind, but still somehow reflected the form and figure of the Monument. Even in those ruffled waters, Dan could easily see the white granite wall, and the deep black fissure of the Blockhead route.

He decided that he really should take a look at that group camp for a few minutes. It would give him a chance to make sure there wasn't any food out anywhere, and it would also allow him to stall a bit, to give Kristen time to get back to camp, if she really was there.

He was surprised to see that the tents were all relatively small—one-, two- and three-man models. Sometimes these large groups packed in a couple of huge safari tents, and everyone slept in one or the other.

Near the main fire ring were two cheap discount store models nestled right up against each other, like shiny plastic Christmas packages under the tree. One was covered with laundry drying in the mountain air.

But as Dan looked around, he picked out another tent farther away, mostly hidden behind a large log. That one looked a bit used, and it was clearly a higher quality as well. And as Dan wandered around the site, he found more. Two were very expensive and high-tech ultra-light tents, tucked into the trees where they were less visible, had it not been for their bright orange colors. It was only after he had finally decided that there was a total of six tents spread around the area that he noticed one more—a well-worn dark blue tent that faded into the dark green of some young firs on the very edge of the rock fall. That one, he thought, is the one that I would want to sleep in.

He liked the way the camp was organized. Food was carefully stacked in bear canisters off to the right. By the fire ring there was a small stack of firewood. Dan even approved of the firewood—nothing too big, nothing for a bonfire, just enough to keep a fire going to take the chill out of the evening. He smiled, thinking that Kristen would have been the one to organize this. He recognized the work of a real pro.

The group had clustered a few large logs near the fire ring and had added in a few folding stools that they had packed in as well, but all things considered, Dan couldn't find much to complain about. Nor could he find much reason to stand or sit around in the vacant campsite. Maybe he should go to the lake and top up his water bottles, just in case.

That's when he heard the voices. He couldn't hear what they were saying, but the tone of the voices was excited, anxious. They were walking down the east side of the lake, along the trail up to Upper Monument Lake, and now he saw them. Two women, walking fast, and making a lot of noise.

One of the women was tall and blond. That would be Kristen, wearing khaki shorts and a pale sky-blue T-shirt, both looking remarkably fresh to be in the back country. She moved with the long, graceful stride of someone who is used to walking and wants to get somewhere fast. As she walked, she was turning her head towards the other woman, maybe encouraging her to keep up.

The other woman was heavier, wearing longer shorts and a bright teal oxford shirt, and as she got closer, Dan could see a dark blue scarf tied neatly around her neck, almost like a cravat. The outfit would have been better suited for a shopping mall than the backcountry. Her steps were shorter and faster, and she was struggling to keep up. And as she got closer, Dan could see and hear that she was crying.

He moved towards the end of the lake, meeting them at the trail junction. When Kristen saw him, she gasped with relief and started talking from thirty yards away.

"Dan!" she gasped. "Okay. There's been an accident. It's over there underneath the cliff. A rock fell and I think he's... I don't think he's in good shape, Dan."

By now the two women were close enough for Dan to see that the woman next to Kristen was sobbing, her make-up running down her face just like the dark streaks in the granite on the cliff behind her. Her lipstick was smeared where she had rubbed her face with the back of her hands. She pulled off the scarf in front of Dan and tried to clean up a bit.

"Where exactly is this?" Dan asked Kristen.

"It's just up by the top end of the lake, less than half a mile. In the middle of some big rocks, at the foot of the Monument." She paused. "You'll find it—the trail goes right in among the rocks. One of the sons is there now. Peter. He was the one climbing." Another pause. "He's pretty upset. I guess a rock fell down... while he was climbing.

His father was down below, and it hit him."

Dan's hand slowly unbuttoned the holster on his belt and reached for his radio to call in. Before speaking into the handheld, he spoke to the two women. "There was an accident earlier up near Sonora Pass, so I am going to call in for support, but I don't know if we can get anyone up here very soon," he said. "Is the dad stabilized? Does he need immediate treatment?"

He looked at Kristen, who slowly and sadly shook her head.

Dan understood. He didn't need any treatment at all.

"Okay," he said. "I'm going to walk up there and see what's going on. And I will call this in so that we can get some support up here when that's available."

He thought for a moment. "What are you going to do?" he asked Kristen.

"Well, we were going to try and hike out of here to get help, but now that you're here..."

"Where is the rest of the group?"

"They've all gone off on their own—each one is supposed to go to someplace different—it's all part of the deal. And they all have lunch with them. They are not supposed to come back to camp until mid-afternoon at the earliest."

Dan thought this over. "Okay, if you would stay in camp and... sort of set that up as a center of operations? I'll go up and see what I can do up here. Once I get through and find out what kind of help we can expect, I'll send... what is his name? Peter?"

Kristen and her companion both nodded.

"I'll send Peter back to camp, too. And he'll be able to tell you, by then, what I've been able to set up on the radio." He took a few steps up the trail, and then stopped.

"Kristen?" His voice and manner asked her to step up close to him.

She nodded and walked back to him, leaving the other woman a few steps further along the trail. Dan leaned towards her to speak quietly. He could smell her—a sort of fresh, floral scent, not one that you would normally find in the mountains, but somehow not completely out of place.

In a far gentler voice than he expected, he said, "Are you going to be okay?"

She nodded and gave him a small, reassuring smile.

"Sure. But this is going to be hard on everyone. I'll get some food going—that will help." And she turned and started walking towards the camp, holding her arm out to envelop the other woman and slowly escort her along. There was a mud stain on the back of the other woman's pants, a long smear down the left leg.

Dan turned and hurried up the trail, hitching his pack up higher on his shoulders, and calling Sara at dispatch on his radio as he walked.

# chapter 2

It was impossible to miss the cluster of huge granite boulders at the top of the lake. They lay like enormous, tumbled chess pieces at the foot of the cliff; left on the ground after the game was done. As Kristen had said, it was just past the upper end of the lake, and Dan could hear the rushing stream off to the left as it rolled by on its way downhill. It was cooler here because of the rocks and the shade they provided.

He thought he saw a brief flash of motion among the rocks, but the trail wound along in a kind of maze through the rock fall. Some of these rocks towered well over his head, and if one of them had fallen it would have crushed a truck, let alone a man. Dan thought back to the other rock, on the other side of the lake. The trail, soft dirt among the hard stones, led him around to the right, then back to the left underneath one of the biggest boulders.

It was only when he got right in among the rocks that he saw the body on the ground in the middle of the trail. It was lying motionless, face down across the trail, and as he got closer, Dan could see a large dark stain of blood on the ground by the head.

He slowed his pace, stopping ten feet from the body on the ground. The top and back of the head was an ugly deep red-black color, as if it had been dipped in paint. But it was more than just painted—there was something wrong with the shape of the head as well. It wasn't quite round. It was hard to tell exactly without getting closer.

It occurred to Dan that it was his job to get closer, to see exactly what had happened. To make sure that the man (and from the bony frame and short haircut, it was obviously a man, an older man) was really dead.

But this wasn't something that you rushed into. Dan stood over the body and noted the worn hiking boots and clothes. The khaki shirt was soft and well-worn. Not the synthetic fibers of modern gear, this one was light cotton. The olive-colored shorts, also cotton, were shorter than is fashionable now, with a cuff at the middle of the thigh. And the boots. Dan had not seen boots like this in a long time: pure leather, with hard, tough soles. The heavy woolen socks extended up out of the boots like dark foam up the legs. This was someone who felt at home in the mountains, and so did his equipment. The pack was faded dark blue nylon, with heavy leather stitched onto the bottom. It was well-worn and not stuffed full. And it looked like that might be the strap for some binoculars around his neck, but they were now out of sight, under his body. Dan gave a quick glance around, but didn't see any sign of the son, Peter.

Dan got down on one knee, leaned forward, and reached out to touch the neck of the dead man, just to make sure he had no pulse. From this distance Dan could see that the rock had simply crushed his skull, and there was a pool of blood in the open cavity. He could see bits of bone around the edges, and he didn't really look too closely at what might have been a bit of brain showing inside.

Dan's hand was just about to touch the man's neck when he heard a loud intake of breath come from behind him. The noise startled him, and he jerked back and spun around to look.

Perched on a rock well above the trail was a rock climber, with his face in his hands. He was sitting on his heels, knees up to his face, on the top of one of the largest boulders. His hands were white with the chalk of a climber, and his rough knees and wiry calves stuck out towards Dan from above. He was deeply tanned, and wore only a thin sleeveless t-shirt and spandex shorts. Thin blond hair stuck out above the hands covering his face. He loomed over the trail like some kind of strange bird.

"Are you Peter?" Dan asked, once his heart began to beat again, at a rate that Dan would not have thought possible without massive exercise.

"Oh God." The man looked at Dan and then nodded. He took a deep, shaky breath and then said, "I killed him. I was up on the wall, way up by that ledge, and I knocked a slab loose."

Another huge sigh. His face was startling, covered with chalk from his hands and smeared with tears. The hands were almost unidentifiable, like some of kind of blend of rock and flesh, hard, calloused, and filthy.

It was an awkward position for a conversation. Dan would have felt better with Peter down at his level, but Peter didn't show any signs of wanting to get off his perch or get closer to the dead body.

"I'm going to just check him out now," Dan said quietly. Somehow he felt calmer explaining to Peter what he was going to do. He turned to the body and then held his hand on the neck, hoping to avoid too much blood, searching for the pulse. There was no pulse. There was enough blood for Dan to realize that he should be careful now with everything else he touched.

He took out his compass from his pocket and held the signaling mirror in front the dead man's mouth and nose. There was no condensation.

Dan turned and quietly faced Peter. "I've called for some help up here, but it's going to be a while before it gets here."

He checked to see if Peter was tracking what he was saying. Peter nodded.

"There's a sheriff who is on his way, hiking in from the trailhead, with a team carrying a litter. There's been a bad accident on the highway, so it will take a little time for everyone to get here."

Peter looked off into the distance. His eyes were already bloodshot, and tears streaked his face. Dan knew that it would be wise to stay here, if only to keep any animals away. But he didn't need Peter to do that. And he thought Peter might be better off with his sister. Dan would almost certainly be better off with Peter somewhere else.

"I don't think there is much you can do here," Dan said. Then he realized that this wasn't true. He should get more information. "Was this someone from your group?" he asked Peter.

Peter nodded, then covered his face again. Through his gnarled and filthy hands, his voice could barely be understood, but Dan did hear him.

"It's my father."

"Okay. Can you tell me his name, and yours?" Dan began to take notes, partly to give some kind of order to the conversation, partly because he would need this information at some point to file his report.

The dead man was Max (Maximillian) Himmel. He lived in San Francisco, but also had residences in Vienna and Florida.

As Peter talked, he seemed to calm down a bit. Peter Himmel lived in Long Barn, above Sonora, when he wasn't climbing something. He did that all over the world.

"Can you tell me what happened?" asked Dan.

It took a while, but the full story slowly came out. Peter had left camp early in the morning, looking to try a new and relatively difficult route up the cliff. The rest of the group was splitting up after breakfast, each heading off to do something different. Peter had slowly worked his way up the face of the cliff, free-climbing, using very little hardware. But at some point, up near the high ledge, he had found an old piton in the rock, and decided to dislodge it to clean up after the people who had left it there.

Dan thought it must have been there a long time. Pitons hadn't really been used for what? Twenty? No, more like thirty years. And he thought that Peter must be quite a climber, if he was doing that wall without hardware. Dan's stomach tightened at the thought of it.

Peter continued. He'd knocked the piton loose and put it in his bag. But as he climbed above the notch where the piton had been, the rock gave way under his foot, and a slab went crashing down below. Out of habit he had yelled a warning, but he really didn't expect that anyone would be below him. And so he kept climbing, finally, after a difficult move, reaching the ledge. He sat down and drank some water, ate an energy bar. He took a few photos of the lake and the valley. The hard part of the climb was over. He was resting there when he looked below and noticed the body laid out below.

He had yelled, and then yelled some more. He had pulled ropes out of his pack and begun to rappel back down the cliff when he heard a scream, and saw Veronica below. He saw her look up at him, and then she yelled something. He yelled down to her that it had been an accident. He saw Veronica leave to get Kristen. And when he finally reached the bottom, his father was dead, and the two women told him to wait there, while they went to get help.

After a few minutes of standing quietly by while Peter suffered, Dan suggested that Peter climb down from his perch and go back to the camp. He had no desire to make Peter hear the next set of radio calls back to base, because those calls were to confirm that there was no hurry.

Peter slowly lifted his pack onto his back, every motion seemingly causing pain. Once the pack was on his shoulders, Peter gave a quick glance at Dan, then shifted his gaze back up at the cliff. After a few moments, he gave a deep sigh and started walking back down the trail towards the lake. After twenty steps he stopped, and Dan thought he was going to turn around and say something, but instead Peter ran his left hand through his hair, pausing for a minute to rest the hand on his neck, before he let it dangle back down along his side. Then he walked off towards camp.

Dan walked back into the rock fall and called dispatch. From that conversation he learned that he would probably be here a few more hours, at least.

Because they were in a wilderness area, they were going to send a team in with a litter. Dan knew that in an emergency, they could fly the chopper into the wilderness, but this wasn't an emergency—there wasn't a chopper in the world that was fast enough to save Max Himmel.

From what Sara at dispatch told him, it sounded likely that Sheriff Cal Healey would get to him first, sometime later this afternoon, because his vehicle was up near the trailhead already. But they were going to send in a team of three more people with the litter. Depending on everything else, that might not be until tomorrow. Dan found a spot to sit, just downhill from the trail, leaned back on his hands, and settled in to wait. An enormous sense of sadness sat with him.

He could hear the creek rushing through the floor of the valley, its water tumbling over the rocks. He could feel the dry, clear air of the mountains, going in and out of his lungs. It seemed important to notice those things—to take the time to realize that he was alive to notice them. He looked up to see an osprey calmly soar high over the trees, sailing down the valley, heading for the lake. It whirled in mid-flight, swooped low over the creek, and landed on a bare branch in a tree at the head of the lake.

Dan could hear an odd sound, a kind of high, piercing noise. He sat up to look around for the source of the noise, and as he did so, the noise stopped. Senses alert, he scanned the area, now hoping to find some kind of explanation. There was nothing he could see that would make that kind of noise. But after a few minutes, he gave up and leaned back again.

The noise began again. And as he sat up, it stopped.

Dan turned and looked at the rock where he was sitting. A tiny blob of flesh-colored plastic and chrome—a hearing aid—lay just near his hand. He moved his hand back to cover it, and the hearing aid squealed in feedback. He picked up the hearing aid, realizing that it had belonged to Peter's father—to the dead man.

He carefully studied it, then dropped it into his shirt pocket, but now he leaned forward. Without really admitting it to himself, he began to scan the ground around him, to see if there was anything else near-by. After a few minutes he found the second hearing aid, nestled up against a granite boulder. He had to get to his feet to collect that one, and once on his feet, he began to take the search more seriously.

A few feet further down the slope, something gleamed from behind a rock. He scrambled down and found a pair of glasses, one lens cracked. Now he was ten feet down the slope, looking back up at the rock fall and the trail. He could just barely see the top of the head on the trail, and above the boulders, the rock wall that Peter had been climbing. The creek was now only fifty feet below him.

Dan stared at the rock face. It looked like a tough climb. Dan had done a little climbing when he was younger, and he understood enough to know that this would have been a serious climb. Even from this closer vantage point, the granite was very clean, very smooth. Peter must be really good. Dan could see a potential route, starting slightly to the right of where he stood, and working up a crack, but then what? There seemed no way to progress from there. He knew that there would be tiny nubs of rock to use, but from here it looked impossible. The tiny ledge at the top was almost invisible from here. From Peter's report, that was where the rock would have come from, he thought.

How far above was that? Six hundred feet? Five hundred? High enough. By the time the rock got down here, it would have been moving with fatal force, ricocheting down the face. For the second time that day, he wondered what kind of impact it would have made. This time it would not have been the heavy thunder of a massive boulder, but a smaller, deadly, crackling descent.

So where was the rock?

Dan tried to imagine it falling, hitting Peter's father, and then what? Straight down the slope? Off to the side? And how far? How fast was it moving? And how big was it? He looked around. There were no obvious candidates from where he stood. He looked at his watch: 12:15. It would be another hour and a half, at least, before Cal showed up.

Dan took a deep breath and walked back up to the dead body. He started walking a calm, deliberate search pattern. He didn't know exactly what rock he was looking for, but there seemed no reason why he couldn't find it.

Besides, he might as well keep busy.

# chapter 3

By the time Cal Healey walked into view, Dan had found the rock.

Dan and Cal had met at a few workshops over the past few years, and Dan recognized the steady pace and slightly rolling gait of the Sheriff immediately. Twenty years ago, maybe only fifteen, Cal had been a pretty good athlete. But the years had added some weight to his 5-11 frame, and a bad knee had added that limp. Cal always looked as if he were carrying a burden slightly heavier than anyone else's. It didn't help that he was carrying the usual paraphernalia of his office, complete with revolver, radio, and handcuffs. Dan knew how much all that weighed, and felt a twinge of pity for the Sheriff.

And Dan knew that Cal wasn't going to like what he had to tell him.

Dan had been watching the trail. As he saw Cal come into view he saw Peter and Veronica Himmel walking behind Cal. Dan walked out of the boulders to meet them. He needed to talk to Cal privately.

Cal was first to speak, in that voice that always seemed to be trying to be just a touch lower in register than was perfectly natural. "Bad accident, huh?"

Dan nodded grimly, then turned to Peter and Veronica. "I know this is going to be hard for you, but there is nothing you can do here," he said. He had to get them out of the way so that he could talk to Cal openly.

"Why don't you go back to the camp and wait for the others? They are going to try and send a litter in here later today, and the Sheriff and I have some things to do to get ready for that."

Peter and Veronica considered this for a moment. Peter looked reluctant, but Veronica pulled on his arm and slowly turned him back down the trail.

Once they were out of earshot, Dan sighed and turned to Cal. "I don't think you're going to like this one, Cal."

"Why is that? Hell, I don't like any accidents." Cal's face wore a rough brush of the short mustache over his lip.

Dan led the way into the boulders of the rockfall. "Let me show you," he said.

They stopped in front of the body, now clearly losing all color, with a huge dark red, almost black splotch of blood on the ground around the head.

"Whew!" Cal exhaled. "That's really ugly. What happened?"

"Well, I've talked to the guy who was climbing up here. Peter—the one you met on your way in." Here Dan pointed up to the cliff above. "He is very upset, and convinced that he dislodged a rock that fell down and killed his father. The guy's name is Peter Himmel, and his father was Max—Maximillian."

"Oh, man," Cal muttered while looking up at the cliff. "Wow."

"Yeah," Dan said grudgingly. He paused.

Cal turned his head away from the cliff and looked back at Dan.

"And?" Cal suggested.

"I found the rock," Dan said. "The rock that killed him. It's right down there." Dan pointed to a spot further down the hillside.

Cal and Dan worked their way through the rockfall to where Dan had left a soft red cotton bandana, marking the spot. Tufts of grass were growing up through the talus—the crumbled mass of broken rocks at the bottom of the slope—filling in the areas between the bigger boulders. The rock was a dark black-brown color, about the size of a cantaloupe. It looked as if it was a blend of pebbles and concrete, harsh and broken. A dark stain showed on top.

"Okay," Cal said cautiously. "So I see the cliff, and I see the body, and the rock. This isn't pretty, but it's pretty clear."

"Well, it would be, except for the rock. It's volcanic."

"Okay..." Cal absorbed this information, then stared back at the cliff. "And the cliff is granite."

There was a long pause while the two men studied the cliff.

Cal was the first to break the silence. "But there is some volcanic stuff up there on the very top of the cliff—a layer on top of the granite."

"Yeah, but Peter said he never made it that far. He said he only got to that ledge up there about three-quarters of the way up. And he said that the rock he knocked loose was a slab. That says granite to me. Volcanic is clumped or round, like this rock. This isn't part of a granite slab."

Cal was still thinking things through. "So what if a piece of that volcanic stuff was stuck on the cliff, somehow hanging on the face? It could have fallen that far, then fell down when this guy broke the slab loose."

Dan realized he was going to have to talk Cal through the whole thought process.

"Look at that cliff. This thing is vertical, clean granite. There is no place for a rock to get hung up until you get up to that ledge. And..."

Cal interrupted. "Well, you can't always tell everything from down here. There may be more cracks and crannies that we can't see from here."

"And now look at where the body is," Dan continued. "If you look up from there to the cliff, there is only a tiny little slot for a rock to fit through—maybe about four feet wide. What are the odds that a rock from the top of a cliff falls a hundred feet, hangs up on a tiny ledge—a ledge that is so small that Peter says he is using some hardware to keep himself on the cliff, then falls another few hundred feet through this tiny opening in the boulders, just at the very moment that this guy is walking through the slot? And it doesn't just hit him. It doesn't just break his arm, or hit his leg. It is exactly the right size of a rock for someone to pick up and either throw or swing. And it hits him exactly on the head, where it would kill him instantly."

"It could happen," Cal said reluctantly, still staring up at the cliff.

"What are the odds?" asked Dan. "Follow the path that rock would have to take. From the ledge, I think any rock would actually fall off to the right. I don't think it would land here at all."

He thrust his chin towards the cliff, then looked at Cal again.

"A bad bounce. Maybe the slab hit something down here and ricocheted—bounced another rock out. That's why they are called accidents," Cal said. "I've had golf shots that sure ended up that way."

"Peter said that this was a very tough, steep section he was climbing. That's why there was an old piton up there. That's a pretty small nook or cranny. And one more thing: Peter was climbing this face. Don't you think that his dad would have been looking up at him to watch? But the rock hit the back of his head, not his face."

"Eh. He could have turned around to look at something else." Cal was not giving in easily. "The guy's got binoculars, maybe he saw a bird."

"And didn't hear Peter yell?" Dan was getting a little frustrated at this point. "He was wearing hearing aids, and they were turned on," he continued. "I found them right here. And if he heard Peter yell, he would have either turned around, or ducked behind one of these huge rocks.

But he didn't. He stayed in exactly the one spot right where that rock could hit him in the back of the head."

Cal's resistance was fading, but he hadn't given in. He bent over to look at the rock again, and turned it over. "This has some white powder on it. Any idea what that could be?"

"Climbing chalk. It was all over Peter's hands when I saw him. They use it so their hands don't slip."

"So if he was climbing and grabbed this rock, it would have chalk on it?"

"Yeah," Dan agreed. They were both silent for a few minutes, and then Cal spoke again.

"And if he weren't climbing, and he touched the rock, it would still have that chalk on it, wouldn't it."

"Yeah," said Dan. "And it would have chalk on it if someone else put chalk on it."

"Shit," said Cal.

That was followed by a long silence. They stood in the middle of the hill, each man with one leg anchored down the slope, the other resting on a rock higher up. Cal was the first to move, grunting slightly as he pushed off the lower leg. They climbed back up to the trail.

"So who else saw anything?" asked Cal, once they were back on the trail.

"I haven't had a chance to talk to anyone else," said Dan. "His sister was the first one to get to the body. She was over at the lake and heard Peter yelling from way up on the cliff. He was rappelling down, yelling his head off, and she ran over here and found… this."

"Do we know when the dad left camp? Because it would take Peter a while to climb that high up on the cliff, wouldn't it?"

Dan agreed. "Probably an hour or more; it's a tough climb. But if the dad left within a few minutes of Peter, this could all have happened before Peter ever got started. Then he climbs up the cliff and knocks a rock off to round out his story."

Cal blew out his cheeks and then let the air escape his lips in a long whoosh of air. "Shit. I guess we should go talk to Peter." He paused. "And maybe talk to his sister, and anyone else who can tell us anything about this… I'm going to take my camera and take as many photos as I can right here. Let's try to document this as well as we can."

"Somebody ought to stay here with the body," Dan suggested. "But we obviously have to try to talk to everybody back at camp." He thought for a moment.

"You've been here a while already. I'm guessing that you've already looked around," Cal offered. Dan nodded in reply. "Then I'll stay here," Cal continued. "I can take a few photos and look around a bit myself. You go talk to the people in camp. Try to keep them from overhearing each other?"

Dan nodded. "If it gets too crowded, I may send somebody out to talk to you…"

"That's fine," Cal smiled. "And if you do, ask them to bring me something to eat. I kind of hurried out here and didn't get lunch."

Dan pulled off his pack and handed Cal a couple of energy bars. As he looked at Cal's disappointed face, he had to laugh a little bit. He turned and headed down the trail. "That's just to get you started. I'll try to send something over once I get to camp."

# chapter 4

When Dan got back to the camp, he found Kristen kneeling on a small bright blue foam pad, slicing up cheese and putting it on a tray on the top of a log by the fire pit. He could smell the soft smoke from the fire that had been built earlier in the morning. Now it was just ashes, but the trace of blue smoke drifted into his nose.

Dan noticed that Kristen's hiking shoes were dusty, but beneath that dust they were a powder blue, matching her shirt. Her clothes showed off her trim figure without seeming to try. She looked up and smiled.

Dan thought it would be better to keep this low key for now, so instead of asking a question, he opened his hands in front of himself and looked around the campsite.

Kristen understood. In a quiet voice she murmured, "Veronica is in her tent." She leaned her head towards one of the nearby cheap plastic tents near the fire pit.

"And Peter?"

"He's down by the lake, pumping some water for us." She paused. "I thought it might be good to give him something to do."

Dan nodded, again impressed with the way Kristen seemed to bring calm and order to things.

"Can I ask you a couple of questions?" he asked.

"Sure."

"Tell me what happened this morning. When did people get up, where did they go, that sort of thing."

Kristen nodded, and stopped to think for a minute. She was particularly attractive when she focused like that, Dan thought. Her eyes seemed somehow more intense. "So I got up first—I usually do. That was about 6:30 or so. I started the fire and put some water on." She paused to think. "By about seven the three boys were all up. They have a hard time sleeping in, although they make it sound as if they are really motivated. And Max, the… father. He was up then, too. Peter, Rafael and Max all had oatmeal, so they could get going quickly. They left about 7:30. Luke wanted bacon and eggs, so he was here longer."

A look passed over Kristen's face that was hard for Dan to interpret. She swallowed, her lips revealing a note of distaste. Then she continued:

"Peter went climbing—he said he was going to climb a new route on the Monument. That's the big cliff over there. I guess you know that. Rafael went fishing. Max left with them both, taking the trail over to the other side of the lake."

"So they all left together?" Dan asked.

"Yes… but Max returned about half an hour later. He always does, to get the girls up."

Dan's look conveyed confusion.

"Everybody here is from one family," Kristen said. "Max… was… the father. And the rest of the group is his kids. They do this every year. It's a tradition. But the boys are always up and at 'em early, and the girls all like to sleep in. And Max had his rules about getting up and doing things every day."

Dan waited, then encouraged her to continue by saying, "So Peter was going to climb the Monument, and Rafael was fishing… and Max was back in camp."

Kristen picked up her story. "When Max got back here, Luke said he was going up the trail that you must have taken this morning, coming down to the lake. He said he was going to get up onto Clark Dome." She paused. "I set everybody up with a sandwich and some dried fruit…"

Dan gave a small tight smile. To Kristen, every one of the family was a different mouth to feed.

She continued, "By the time he left, most of the others were up. Max had gone around to all of the tents and made sure everyone was awake and getting dressed." She nodded to one of the brightly colored cheap tents near the fire. "Gloria and Veronica were the last up. They were up late last night drinking, and they were hurting this morning." She pointed to a small tent way up under the trees and said, "That's Rafael's over there…"

"So when did Max leave again? And how many people are here?" asked Dan.

"Well, there are supposed to be eight: Max and his seven kids. But one of the kids isn't here." She counted them off as she pointed her way around the tents, starting at the expensive ones far under the trees. "Peter, and then Luke. Rafael over there. Gloria and Veronica right here. That's Gabriela next to them, in her own tent. Max was over there, by those logs." She indicated with her thumb a small blue tent away from the rest, nestled in among a stand of trees. "And that's me, over there."

"Okay," Dan said. "So Peter and Rafael leave early. When did Max and the others leave? And what was Max planning to do this morning?"

"Well, he has to organize everyone, so he did that," Kristen replied. "So, let's see... Peter and Rafael early—I think Rafael said he was going to go up to the creek above the lake. Max always hikes and watches the birds; that's his big passion. He waited until everybody was up—to make sure they didn't just sit around in camp. Veronica was going to swim in the lake or something—that wasn't very clear. And I think Gloria was going to take some photos of wildflowers. She packed a big lunch. That girl likes to eat. Those two left together. Gabriela just said she was going on a hike... didn't say where, I don't think..." She paused, then came back to Dan. "So Max was the last to leave, because he had to make sure that everyone else had left. That's the deal. I'd guess he left here about nine, and said he was going on a hike—I think he wanted to do some bird watching. He was a big birder."

"He had to make sure everyone else had left?" Dan gave her a puzzled look.

"That's the deal," she said. "He insists on it. They all come up here; they all have to camp together. They have a meeting every night about their family businesses, like a board of directors meeting. And every day they have to go out and do something interesting and different. Each one of them—that's the deal."

Dan's expression didn't change, but he raised his eyebrows at her.

Kristen shrugged her shoulders. "Those are the rules. Max makes them. He is the father and the boss, and if you don't play by his rules, you don't get to be part of the family business." She waited for Dan's reaction. While he thought this over, she continued, "It's weird."

Dan agreed that it was weird. "Reminds me a bit of my dad," he said. "Thank God he didn't have enough money for it to matter..."

Kristen waited for him to continue, but Dan looked away, towards the lake. "Max really loves these mountains," she finally interrupted his thoughts. "He really wants his family to take time to enjoy them, too.

It's just weird that he makes it into this whole expedition, with rules and everything. But it could be worse—he could force them to live in his house or in New York or something."

"Yeah," Dan said slowly. He was thinking about how the family members must react to this trip. "So what time did he leave camp today?"

"I'd guess it was after nine. He left right after Gloria and Veronica walked out together. She's the one who probably resists this the most... or Gloria. Well, no—there is the one daughter who refuses to play the game at all. She isn't here. Sophie. But for the ones that are here, Veronica and Gloria seem to be the most... imposed upon. They are always the last to leave camp. Once he made sure they were up and out of camp, he left again to go back to his bird watching."

"Okay," Dan looked up from his notes to repeat the details. "So Max leaves after nine, right about the same time as the two women. And by then everyone else is out on the trail—or at least out of camp. And when do you hear about the accident?"

"Once everybody left, I cleaned up the place," Kristen answered. "Maybe half an hour at most? And then I had a cup of tea." She smiled apologetically. It was really an endearing expression, Dan thought. "It's my one vice up here... but that's when I heard the yelling. So maybe ten o'clock? Something like that? I didn't know what was going on—I thought maybe it was just an argument or something."

She stopped and looked at him. "There were a lot of those last night, at the board meeting... anyway, it wasn't until Veronica got back here about ten or ten-thirty that I found out what had happened..."

She looked expectantly at Dan. His face was lost in concentration. "What are you thinking?" she asked.

Dan tried to downplay her question. "I'm just putting all this together so that I write the accident report. Where people were, what they were doing. Who was nearby. That sort of thing."

Kristen looked as if she didn't quite believe him but wasn't going to make an issue out of it. But she knew he wasn't being completely open with her. He could see that in the way she looked at him, and he was sorry. He really wanted to explain that away... but realized that he couldn't. Not in this situation.

"What did Veronica say?" he asked.

"She was very upset." Kristen looked over at Veronica's tent. "She was crying, and she said that somehow Peter had killed her father. She insisted that I come and look... I didn't know what to do, but I went over there. Once we got there, I saw there was nothing we could do. I brought Veronica back here and was going to hike out for help when we saw you."

"I guess I know the rest," Dan added. He looked up at her and nodded. "This is really helpful, thanks..." He looked at her, with the sunlight through the trees sparkling in her hair. "Thanks. I think I'll go talk to Peter now."

He took a few steps towards the lake, and then remembered Cal.

"Oh—Kristen? Sheriff Healey is over on the other side of the lake, with the body. He was wondering if you had anything to eat. I guess he missed lunch today."

Kristen nodded. "Sure, I can take him something. We have lots here." She paused. "What about you? Have you eaten?"

Dan smiled sheepishly. "I had a couple of energy bars in my pack," he admitted.

"I'll leave something here for you, too. I'll just put it in the first bear box."

Dan muttered something about not wanting to be any trouble.

Kristen ignored him.

As he walked down to the lake, Dan did the math in his head. It would have taken Peter around half an hour to get to the base of the Monument. That was 8:30. And then at least an hour to climb up to the top. The earliest he could do that would have been about 9:30. And he said he spent some time up there first, taking photos, before he noticed the body. So that was about 9:45 or so. Which was just before Kristen heard the yelling. But if Max didn't leave camp until nine or later, he wouldn't have been at the base of the cliff until about 9:30.

Which would be when Peter might have knocked a rock off.

Okay. So maybe it was an accident after all.

But there was no way that rock could fall and hit Max. Not from way up there.

# chapter 5

Dan followed the use trail through the trees as it led down to the lake. These days every campsite in the Sierra had a trail like this, where campers had worn a path to the best spot to use their water filter. As he walked, he could see the sun glistening off the water of the lake ahead. On a quiet morning the lake would be a perfect mirror for the towering cliff on the other side, but the mid-afternoon breezes dappled the surface now so that each wave caught a bright flash of sun. And at 8,000 feet, the sunlight was almost pure white, without any of the copper or gold tints that would come later in the afternoon.

Peter was sitting on a rock, surrounded by the paraphernalia of the water filter and bottles. One foot was on a rock that stuck out just inches above the water, and he had propped three or four water bottles around him. He was staring off into space, his arms slowly and mechanically working the pump handle back and forth. Dan knew the motion well.

He didn't want to startle Peter, so he cleared his throat a bit as he got closer.

Peter didn't turn around.

"How's it going?" Dan asked.

Peter shrugged, then continued pumping.

Dan sat quietly for a few minutes, letting Peter get used to the idea of conversation.

"I'm sorry, but I need to ask a few more questions, Peter, so that I can write up a report," he said. "Do you mind?"

Peter shook his head. He had filled up one big water bottle, and now moved another into position. Dan reached out to take the full bottle and put its cap on, then placed the bottle next to three others that were lined up on shore. There were three more to fill.

Dan found a more or less flat rock to sit on and eased his lanky body down onto it. His knees, still a bit sore from the long descent earlier in the day, quietly let him know that they were still with him, and still resentful. Dan let out a small groan as he sat.

Peter looked over at him, then back out to the lake.

Dan had learned, over the years, that the best way to ask questions was to wait. It was like fly fishing: if you beat the water with your fly, you usually scared away most of the fish. Put it out there. Let it sit there. Let the fish get used to it. And then, slowly, they would come. Dan tossed out his fly, and sat back to wait.

"Peter, could you just talk me through your day today? From when you got up to when you got to the top of the cliff over there? What happened? Can you help me understand it?"

Peter gave a huge sigh, and then waited. So did Dan. Finally, in a dull monotone, Peter began to run through his day. He got up with Rafael and Luke. And his dad. Ate a quick breakfast and hiked over to the base of the Monument. He wanted to try a new route up the face that he had seen the day before.

Dan asked about the time.

"I was on the wall by about 8:30, but didn't really start the climb until about ten minutes later, 8:40. The first section was pretty easy, but I was worried about a pitch higher up. I spent some time thinking about the best way to get over to my route, so that took me a little longer that it should have."

Dan realized that for Peter, life was about doing things well, doing things fast. He kept track of everything. Dan recognized that, partly because he saw that same character in himself. He liked to know where he was on the trail, and time and distance were important.

"Once I figured that out, I was doing great," Peter continued. "It really was great climbing—clean rock, just beautiful. Pure, clean Sierra granite." He paused to look across the lake at the cliff, staring for quite a few seconds. For a moment, Dan thought that he might be looking for another route to try. Then Peter continued.

"Do you see that ledge up on the cliff?" he asked Dan.

Dan stared across at the white granite.

Peter pointed with his hand still holding the pump. "Follow that dark stain up the right side, and then there is notch... a sideway fissure?"

Dan nodded. "Yeah, okay..."

"It looks pretty vertical from here, but there is plenty of room to sit up there, once you get over the overhang. It's a hairy move, but once you get onto the ledge, you are done. It's amazing to be up there."

"So that's where you were when you saw your dad?"

Peter nodded.

"And where did you find the piton? Where did the slab come loose?"

Again Peter sighed, and waited before he answered.

"Maybe fifteen or twenty feet below the ledge," he replied. "I was following that vertical crack. Some pretty good jams in there, and I was thinking about that last move, over to the ledge. I was just kind of hanging there, thinking, when I saw the pin—the piton. It must have been there for a long time." He looked at Dan for confirmation, and the ranger nodded.

"I thought it would be a nice thing to do, to clean up the rock," Peter went on. "I didn't have a hammer, but I found a nice spot for my left foot, and tied into a chock I set in the crack. That way I could use both hands on the thing. I threaded a loop of rope through it and started working it back and forth. It didn't take much to get it to loosen up. So I just wiggled it around, and it popped free... I thought, 'Great—that's my good deed for the day.'"

Dan couldn't help smiling to himself. "So then you went on up over the ledge."

"Peter shook his head. "No... I was still thinking about how to do that. I rested there, since I had a good spot, studied it a moment, and figured out how I was going to get over that. I had a couple of really good handholds as I worked up, and I was going to try to get a little lift with my right foot... I pushed against the slab where the piton had been... I guess I must have loosened it up a bit. It gave way and fell off down below."

Dan waited for him to continue.

"I yelled 'rock' down there, but I knew there was nobody else out here." He paused. "I thought I knew... I didn't think anyone was there."

"How big was this slab that fell off?" asked Dan. "Could you tell?"

"Well, I was hanging there... and the adrenaline was pumping pretty good. But I think it was a couple of feet across. It wasn't like a whole section of the rock had come loose. Just a flake, maybe the size of a backpack, only thinner, like six inches thick?"

Dan carefully wrote in his notepad. He would remember this perfectly well, but he wanted the time to think, and he wanted to give Peter time to talk. When he was done, he looked up expectantly at Peter.

"So that's it," Peter said. "I could hear the flake pocking and crashing down below. That went on for a few seconds. After I made sure I was okay, I moved on up, and got on the ledge. It was easier than I thought—or maybe I just had a lot of adrenaline by then. But it was easy." Peter was clearly proud of his skills; there was no hiding that tone in his voice.

"What did you do once you got to the ledge?" asked Dan.

Peter thought for a minute. "It was amazing… I just sat there. That was a very tough route I took. I don't think there are very many people who have done that, and I wanted to savor it a bit. I sat there and just looked out over the lake and the valley… the sun was warm by then, and I drank some water, and ate something. Mainly I just sat there."

"Did you check to see where that rock had fallen?" Dan asked.

Peter nodded. "Yeah, but I couldn't see anything. I could see where I thought it went, but it was all just talus down there. It was all just white granite, and that flake was one of about million rocks that had fallen down there. I couldn't see anything else."

Dan looked puzzled. "So you couldn't see your dad then?"

"I don't know," Peter shrugged his shoulders. "I wasn't really looking where he was… I was looking more straight down, where I thought it had gone… but I only checked for a second or two. I didn't see anything, and I wasn't worried about anything,"

"And did you see anyone else?" Dan asked.

"No, not really. I mean, I could see our campsite from there, so I guess I saw the cook there…" Peter replied.

By this time Peter had filled all the water bottles and had carefully put away the pump—red cap on the output barb, black cap on the intake barb, intake hose in one baggie, output hose in the other one. It was something he had done a hundred times, Dan could see.

"So when did you see your dad?"

"It must have been half an hour later. I was trying to decide where I would rappel down, and I was looking for the trail, way below. I could see it along the lake… and then where it went into the boulders. That's when I saw my dad. It was hard to see… there were some shadows, and the boulders kind of blocked my view. I pulled out my binoculars, and then I saw him. I was sure it was him. And I just started yelling and screaming. I set up my rappel and made it partway down the cliff. That's when I started yelling again. And I think Veronica finally heard me, or finally decided to do something… she got there first. That's when I knew it was dad."

Dan stuck out his hand towards the bottles. "Can I help you get those back to camp?" he asked Peter.

Peter handed him two of the bottles and then, when he saw Dan hold out his hand again, added the water filter.

Given Peter's explanation of what happened, there was little question in Dan's mind that the rock that Peter had knocked loose wasn't the rock that killed his father. It couldn't be, not if Peter was talking about a flake of granite.

He started to lead the way back to camp, reflecting his training as a ranger. He was used to leading hikes. But he was now sure that this was not an accidental death. He was sure it was murder. And as he led the way back to camp, the hairs on his neck stood up, and he got an icy chill on his back. He stepped aside on the trail, as if to take one more look at the lake and the cliff. Peter kept walking, taking the lead back to camp. Dan let Peter go first.

And Dan, after a brief shiver, followed him.

"Why don't they just use a chopper? You mean they are going to just carry him out of here?" Luke seemed suddenly distressed, as much by that idea as by the death of his father.

"This is a wilderness area. We don't use choppers in here if we can help it."

"So those guys are going to have to carry him down that trail?"

Dan nodded. "Yeah, that's how we do it."

"I guess they know what they're doing," Luke added, then looked at Kristen. "If they don't need any help, maybe I'll just stay here in camp."

Kristen moved over to the nearest tent, and tapped on one of the poles. "Veronica?" she said, "Luke is back. Why don't you come out now? I think it would help."

From inside the tent, there was a small response, and Dan could see movement inside.

As he started to leave, Kristen stopped him. "Wait, wait. You have to take your lunch."

She bent over the food canisters and opened them up, pulling out a variety of bags and packages.

"Hey, I don't need all that!" Dan smiled.

"Just wait," Kristen said. "This won't take long."

She fussed with the bags and laying out the food on the log. It seemed to take forever, but about the time that he heard the zipper from Veronica's tent make its squeal, Kristen handed him a bag with an assortment of goodies. "There should be enough here for both of you—even Cal," she smiled.

Dan thanked her and walked out of the campsite, hearing Veronica's voice talking to Luke as he left. He wondered why Kristen had stalled him until Veronica had come out of her tent.

# chapter 7

Dan walked back around the lake, but before he got to the junction, he met a young woman racing up the trail, clearly out of breath and out of sorts.

Short, with short, cropped dark hair and the body and energy of a gymnast, the young woman was gasping for breath as she walked towards him. He was surprised to see lipstick and makeup on her face, which was dripping with sweat.

"What's happened?" she confronted him. "Who's been hurt?"

Dan held his hands out in front of himself, as much to protect himself from the energy radiating out of the young woman as anything else.

"There's been an accident," he began. The trite words were also a way of calming things down, falling into a kind of ritual that they could both understand.

"I know that. I met the rescue team," she responded quickly and with a touch of impatience. "Who is it? What's happened?"

Dan was aware that the conversation was veering out of control, and tried to rope it in. "Are you a member of the family?"

The young woman stared at him, and then snapped, "I am Gabriela Himmel. I am Max Himmel's daughter, and I am the general manager of his business operations. Now what the hell happened?"

She glared at Dan, her mouth slightly quivering.

Dan took a deep breath. "I am afraid your father was apparently hit by a rock in the head, Ms. Himmel. He did not survive the impact. I am sorry."

She stopped, staring up at the ranger with her mouth slightly open. "He's dead?" Her eyes drifted off to the side as she considered the news.

"I'm sorry," Dan repeated.

Gabriela took a deep breath, then looked back at Dan, fully focused now. "Where is everybody? Where's my dad?"

"I think most of your family is back at the camp now," Dan replied. Pointing to the left, he said, "The SAR team is up this trail, near the head of the lake. That's where your father was… hit."

Gabriela's gaze followed Dan's arm towards the end of the lake, then riveted back on his face. "Who knows about this?" she asked. "My father is a very important businessman. An industry leader." She paused to think. "I would like to ask you to allow us to announce this to the press, when we are ready to do that. Is that possible?"

Dan held up his hands and shrugged. "I don't have any control over that," he said. "I can tell you that I won't be speaking to any newspapers or anything… but I don't think I can control what happens in town."

Gabriela considered this for a minute. "Where are they taking him?"

"I think they'll take your dad to the county hospital in Sonora," Dan said. "At least, that's my guess."

Gabriela checked her watch, then looked back at Dan. "How long will that take?"

"I'd guess it will take them at least a couple of hours to get back to the trailhead, maybe more. And another hour back into Sonora. They won't get there before 7:30 or 8. And it could take a lot longer."

Gabriela thought for a moment, then looked at her watch again. "They won't do anything with this tonight. It's a small paper… a weekly… okay. I am going to the camp," she announced. "You said everyone was there?"

"I saw Peter, Luke and Veronica there." He checked the names off his fingers to keep track. "I don't know where the others are."

"Gloria won't be far away; she never is. Rafael is fishing; he won't get back until dinner, at the earliest." She paused once more. "I am going to the camp. If you see Rafael, please ask him to go there ASAP."

Dan agreed.

She looked at him. "Thank you," she said. It was clear to Dan that it was not only an expression of gratitude. It was also a dismissal.

He watched her stride powerfully up the trail, then turned around and continued towards the SAR team.

He got there just as they were finishing their preparations and getting ready to leave. Dan noted with some satisfaction that the three guys in the team were all reasonably big and strong. Sometimes he worried about some of kids they sent on these missions. He wasn't sure that they had the body strength to do the job. These three were clearly up to the task.

Dan handed the lunch bag to Cal and turned to the men clustered around the litter.

"Hi, guys. Thanks for the help. Did you guys notice anything that I didn't see?" he asked.

Cal shook his head. "Blunt force trauma to the back and top of the head. No other injuries that we could see. I'm thinking that death would have been pretty instantaneous."

The members of the SAR team agreed. Dan noted that one had a florid tattoo that covered most of his arm. "Time of death?" he asked.

The tattooed arm responded. "We can't say for sure; we're not coroners. Body temp wasn't down much, but in this weather it wouldn't drop much. Sometime this morning?"

"Yeah, we know that. We're just trying to figure this one out," Dan said. He looked at Cal. "The family would like to keep this quiet for a bit." He indicated the body of Max Himmel. "He was a pretty important guy, so this is going to affect his business, I guess."

Cal snorted. "It sure is! So what do they expect us to do?"

"I didn't promise anything. But they would prefer it if we didn't call anybody about it."

"Hell, I'm not going to call anybody about this!" He turned to the SAR team. "Are you guys going to call anybody about this guy? His family would like a little privacy."

All three members of the SAR team mumbled their agreement, shaking their heads.

"Okay, are you guys good to go?" Cal asked them.

"We want to get out of here before it gets too dark," the young man at the head of the litter replied. His name tag said his name was Adam. "Once we get over the hump here, that downhill isn't going to be any fun with this stretcher, and it's going to be a lot harder if we can't see."

"Go!" Cal said, stepping off the trail to clear the way.

"Thanks, guys," Dan said.

He stood next to Cal, off the trail, as the two litter carriers grunted the litter into position and started down the trail. Adam, the last to leave, took a quick look around, picked up a couple of wrappers from the ground, and followed them. As he left, he handed the dead man's binoculars to Cal. "The family may want these," he said.

Cal and Dan watched them go, then Cal shook the bag of food.

"I am starving here. Is there any reason to get back to that camp right now, or do we have time to sit down and eat something?"

Dan chuckled quietly. "We have time to eat," he said, "and I have a few things to tell you, as well."

"Good," Cal said. "You talk while I eat." He sat down on a rock and ripped open the bag of food. "Damn… there's good stuff here."

"Yeah, Kristen made that for us," Dan said. As he watched, Cal bit into a sandwich, getting almost a quarter of the sandwich in his mouth in one bite. "And I do want to stress that she made it for us." Dan emphasized the last word.

Cal, mouth full of food, handed the bag back to Dan.

"Hey, if you want something, you better take it now," he mumbled through a mouthful of food. "I won't promise you there's going to be anything left if you wait!"

Dan took the bag and sat on a rock, facing Cal. Cal was right; there was a lot of food in there: another sandwich, a baggie full of Cheezits, some dried fruit, a baggie of trail mix, and a couple of cookies. He pulled out the sandwich and peeled it open. Salami, some shaved parmesan cheese, and both mayonnaise and mustard.

"This looks great!" he said.

"Oh yeah, it is," Cal replied, taking another huge bite of his sandwich. "Hey, hand me some of those Cheezits."

While Cal wolfed down his lunch, Dan took a more leisurely approach, bringing Cal up to speed on his conversations with Kristen, Peter and Luke between bites.

Cal dug back into the bag to pull out the trail mix, then looked back at Dan. "So the way you figure it, Peter was up on that ledge about 9:30, and Luke saw him there, huh?"

"Yeah," Dan replied. He thought it over for a few minutes. "I may be wrong about this whole thing, Cal. It made sense to me when I sat here and thought it out. But there is no way that Peter could have killed his dad with that rock. At least not intentionally, not from that ledge."

Cal grunted his agreement and opened up the lunch bag again, looking for the dried fruit and cookies. He triumphantly pulled out a box of raisins and a chocolate chip cookie, then looked back at Dan. "So maybe this was just a really weird accident?"

Dan was unwilling to concede the point but couldn't make any sense of the rest of it. "I guess I'm going to talk to the rest of the family. My gut tells me I'm right. I still think that this wasn't an accident, but it doesn't look like it was Peter who did it. There are a lot of people up here…"

"That's going to take some time," Cal suggested, "if you're planning on talking to them all."

"I think I have to, at this point," Dan said. "If this isn't the weirdest accident in history, then somebody had to be here, right here, about 9:30, with a rock in their hand. And right now, the only thing I know is that Peter was up on the ledge, and Luke was over on Clark Dome."

"It's hard to imagine one of the daughters crashing in a skull like that, don't you think?" Cal responded. "Do you think Luke could be lying? Maybe they're in it together?"

"From what I saw at the camp, they're not great fans of each other, so I think that's unlikely."

Cal took this in. "Unless they were faking that?"

Dan took a deep breath and stared out across the lake. The peace and beauty of the Sierra seemed somehow artificial now. The bright sunlight on the water hurt his eyes. It was hard to remember how beautiful the lake was this morning.

He looked back at Cal. "What a mess. You know, this started out to be a pretty nice day for me." And he told Cal about seeing the bear on the trail.

Cal wiped his hands off on his handkerchief, then took off his sunglasses and rubbed his eyes. He leaned back against the rock and crossed his arms over his chest. As he gazed out over the lake, he said to Dan, "I had the SAR team leave me a couple of blankets." He waited, but didn't get a response from Dan. "It's not supposed to get too cold tonight, so I figured that I could stay around and help you."

"This is a pain in the ass," Dan said. "So thanks. I can loan you a jacket, too."

Cal smiled thinly. "Welcome to my world, Ranger Courtwright."

As the two men sat thinking, a hiker appeared on the far end of the trail, walking back down towards the lake, carrying a fly rod. Powerful and stocky, he was staring off towards the stream as he hiked. A hat and short, dark beard made it hard to see his face.

"Wanna bet that's somebody we have to talk to?" Cal asked, not moving from his position.

"Yeah… that's gotta be Rafael."

The fisherman suddenly noticed the two men, stopped in his tracks, then turned sharply around and went back up the trail into the alders along the stream.

Cal and Dan exchanged looks. Cal sat up and handed the empty lunch bag to Dan. "Looks like maybe we should go have a chat with him."

Dan held up the empty lunch bag and stared at Cal.

Cal laughed. "Hey, you didn't seem hungry!" he said as he stood up and started walking up the trail to where Rafael had disappeared.

Dan stuffed the empty bag into his pants pocket and followed him up the trail.

# chapter 8

"This reminds me of looking for a golf ball." Cal had stopped on the trail, trying to identify where Rafael had left it to head down to the river. The alders grew well above their heads, hiding both the stream and the next stretch of trail. They could hear the water rushing by, but could not see into the dense thicket. "Was it about here?"

Dan turned around and looked back at their lunch spot. "I'll head to the creek from here. Why don't you follow the trail up a ways, then cut over to the creek. That way we'll have him somewhere in between us."

Cal thought this over. "You know, if Peter was up on the cliff, and somebody hit his dad with a rock... the best candidate for that right now is this guy. I'm not sure we should go bushwhacking through these alders without knowing where he is and what he's doing. And I am damn sure we shouldn't split up and wander around in here looking for him. That's asking for a problem." He pulled his gun out of his holster, checking the safety, and looked at Dan.

"How about this?" Dan suggested, looking hard at Cal's pistol. "You go ahead up the trail and work your way back down along the stream. I'll wait out in the clearing here, and if he does come out, I'll let you know. And I will keep my distance."

Cal thought it over. "Is there any chance this guy is armed? Because I don't like this very much. This guy could be twenty feet away from us in these bushes, and we wouldn't know it."

"Hang on, Cal." Dan turned towards the steep rubble behind them and started to climb up on the blocks of broken granite. Within a few minutes he was well above the level of the trail and looking for a solid boulder to stand on. He took a big step up onto a flat boulder. It rocked slightly under his weight, then rocked back as he shifted his balance. Stable now, he straightened up and began to look out over the stream and the dense alders that surrounded it.

In the stream beyond the alders, he could see the top of Rafael's fly rod, slowly arcing back and forth, the fly line curving in delicate arcs behind it. He could just make out Rafael's head through the tops of the branches.

He called down to Cal. "He's fishing," he said, and pointed to give the Sheriff a direction to follow. "He's out on a rock in the middle of the creek." And he waved his hand to suggest that Cal go a bit further up the stream.

Dan followed Cal's progress through the alders. The Sheriff was working through the bushes. At times Dan could see Cal pause, looking for a way to push through a particularly thick section, then saw those branches shake and quiver as Cal pushed through them. He saw Rafael stop fishing and turn around at one point, looking for what was causing the disturbance, and for an instant he considered calling out to Cal, to warn him. But then Rafael returned to his fishing, floating a cast downstream, holding the rod high as the fly drifted.

Cal struggled out onto the edge of the stream and quickly located Rafael, about twenty yards downstream. It seemed to Dan that Rafael was determined not to allow the Sheriff to interrupt him, but eventually he saw the fly rod dip, and Rafael turn around and face Cal.

When Dan saw that, he hopped off his rock and clambered down the jumbled rocks, across the trail, and tried to follow Cal's path through the alders.

They were thick and growing out like oversized clumps of monster grass. The bigger branches were more than two inches thick, and even the smaller ones were so dense and flexible that it was a continual struggle to work through them. Dan found himself going no faster than Cal. He climbed over one branch, pushed another out of the way, and ducked through an opening, only to find the way blocked by more alders. He could hear the stream burbling in front of him, and now he heard voices. One higher pitched, and angry. And Cal's voice lower, and calmer.

Dan hurried forward, ripping through the alders, scraping a knee on a broken branch. He twisted in pain and pushed on.

Dan burst through the last of the alders, then realized that he had no place to put his feet on the edge of the stream. He lunged for a rock about two feet out into the water, landed on it with his right foot, and felt it tilt underneath him. He lost his footing and plunged forward, straight into the water. He fought to regain his footing, standing up to his knees in the stream, and then climbed up on a rock, his boots and socks soaked.

He looked up to see both men staring at him. Rafael's face froze, contorted in fury. Cal, pistol in his hand, glanced quickly behind to check on Dan, then back to Rafael.

"Glad to see you could make it," he muttered over his shoulder to Dan.

"Shit!" Rafael Himmel spit the word out. "You guys really know how to fuck up a stream." He turned away from the two men and slowly started to reel in his fly line, shaking with rage. As he did so, Cal started talking to him again.

"Just calm down. We got called up here for an emergency," he was saying. "And we need to talk to you about what happened today."

Rafael didn't reply. When most of the line was back on his reel, he lifted up the rod and caught the fly in his bare hand. He tucked the rod under his arm, and quickly snipped the fly off the line, tucking it into his hatband.

Dan decided that he was already wet, so there was no need to worry about rock hopping across the steam at this point. He waded up to Cal, then waded through the water to the shore, across from the rock where Rafael was standing.

Rafael glanced at him for a moment, then finished reeling in his line and began to take apart his fly rod, pulling it into sections. He did so silently, without making eye contact with either of the other two men. He was done fishing, at least for a while. For an instant Dan thought that he was going to hop off to the other side of the stream. Instead, Rafael turned toward him and started walking right at Dan, his fly rod in one hand and wading staff in the other.

Dan backed up into the alders, found a place that was a bit of a clearing, and waited. Cal immediately spoke up. "Hold it! I need you to stay where you are for a couple of minutes," he said. "Just stand where you are and let us ask a few questions, okay?"

Rafael slowly looked back up the stream to Cal, then turned on the rock to face him completely. With chin out and shoulders hunched, he stared Dan straight in the face, and between clenched teeth, said, "What?"

Rafael's short black beard framed his square face. He was shorter than his brothers, Dan noticed. And his body was stocky, with almost no neck. He was dressed in a red and black plaid flannel shirt and brown jeans, with a fishing vest hanging loosely over the shirt. A broad-brimmed Australian hat, brim pulled up on one side, completed the look.

With Cal balancing on a rock in the stream, and holding his pistol aimed at Rafael, Dan thought it would be a good idea to step in and handle the questions himself.

"Can you tell us what you did this morning?" he asked Rafael. "What time you left camp, and where you went?"

Rafael thought this over, then turned back to Dan and slowly recounted his morning. "I left camp after breakfast. My brother and I walked up here, more or less together. He went up there," Rafael glanced up at the cliff, "and I started fishing. I fished up to the meadow all morning, then ate lunch up there." Rafael paused, as if trying to decide how much detail to provide. "It was the middle of the day, so I waited a bit. Then I fished back down here."

Cal asked, "So once you left Peter, did anybody see you up here?"

Rafael stared at Cal. "Do you mean, do I have an alibi?" He shook his head. "I like to fish alone. Do you want to explain what this is all about?"

Neither Dan nor Cal wanted to show their cards yet. Cal asked, "Did you catch any fish?"

"Some," Rafael replied guardedly.

"And did you see anyone else?"

Rafael thought a bit, then said, "I saw Peter up there." He pointed to the cliff again. "Maybe he can tell you what I was doing. And there was some guy in camo climbing around on the rocks below this morning. I have no idea who he was or what he was doing. I didn't see any reason to pay attention to him, either."

Cal and Dan exchanged a quick glance. "What time was that?" Cal asked.

"I don't know. I don't pay much attention to time when I am fishing. That's kinda the point. I don't know, maybe I'd been fishing about an hour?"

"And where did you see this guy?"

Rafael pointed with his fly rod. "Over there, underneath the Monument. I didn't really see much, I just noticed that someone was moving around down there."

"And he was wearing camouflage?" Cal asked.

Rafael nodded. "Yeah. Pretty good, too. If he hadn't been moving, I wouldn't have noticed him."

"Okay," said Cal. "You're saying 'he.' Are you sure it was a man?"

Rafael shrugged. "No. But I don't know many women who wear camo."

Cal looked at Dan, letting him know it was his turn.

"When you were walking back on the trail, just now, when you saw us, you stopped and suddenly turned around. Why?" Dan asked.

A flicker of concern flashed over Rafael's face, then he stared into the water and replied. "I fish because I like to be alone," he said. "And when I saw you guys… well, you ruined that."

Dan asked Rafael if he was going back to camp now.

"I don't know." Rafael was still staring into the water, not making eye contact with either man. "I may just sit here for a while."

"But you're still planning to eat dinner there tonight?"

Rafael nodded. Dan looked at Cal. Cal shrugged. "I guess we'll see you there," Cal said.

As they walked towards the trail, Dan kept thinking about the conversation with Rafael. Something bothered him about how the fisherman had responded. He stopped in the middle of the alders, then turned back to look at Rafael.

Rafael was staring at Dan. When he realized Dan was staring back, he quickly looked away.

What was he thinking? Dan turned to work his way up out of the alders, when he noticed a small bag on the ground, tucked into the roots of an alder. He looked back at Rafael again, and realized that the man on the rock was still watching him.

"Is this yours?" Dan asked.

"What is it?" Rafael asked, not meeting Dan's gaze, his face a mask of ambivalence.

Dan reached over and picked up the bag. As he picked it up, he suddenly knew what was inside. He held it up for Rafael to see.

Rafael didn't respond immediately. He stared at the bag, and then at Dan Courtwright. Finally, he nodded.

"Do you mind if I see what's inside?" Dan asked.

Rafael shrugged.

Dan pulled open the flap and looked inside. Gleaming silver bodies met his gaze. Beautiful trout. How many of them? He didn't want to count.

"How many did you get?" he asked the fisherman.

Rafael shrugged again, then added, "I don't know. Five or six."

Dan looked into the creel. He guessed there were at least six fish in the bag, probably more. "The limit is five, you know."

Rafael stared at Dan for a few seconds, then answered, "I didn't keep any yesterday."

Dan thought about this. It didn't matter how many Rafael had caught or kept yesterday. The law said the limit was five fish per day, and a maximum of five in possession. He could easily write a ticket, and the fine would probably be $100 a fish or more.

He heard a movement in the alders behind him, and Cal pushed his way through the thicket towards him.

"What's going on?" Cal asked.

Dan put the bag back under the roots where he had found it, and turned to walk out with Cal. "I'll explain later," he said.

Once back on the trail, Dan told Cal about the fish.

"So that's why he turned around on the trail and lit out on us, huh?" Cal asked.

Dan nodded. "I don't know if that's the whole story... but it might be some of it."

"He's an angry man," Cal noted.

Dan, pushing an alder branch out of his face and he walked back to the trail, didn't argue with that. He was angry, too, about the fish. But he also didn't see much point in writing the guy up for a couple of trout, not on the day that his father died.

# chapter 9

Back on the trail, Dan and Cal discussed next steps. "We don't have a murder right now," Cal said. "What we have is some odd information, and a weird coincidence. But we don't know if the guy was murdered, or if he just got hit by a rock."

"We know he got hit by the rock," Dan said. "We just don't know if anyone was holding that rock when it hit him." They had bagged up the rock and sent it into town with the SAR team. "Do you think a lab will be able to get anything off the rock?"

"I have no idea. If that rock was thrown, then maybe it has some DNA on it. I don't know. But we also don't really even have a motive yet, either. What we have is an odd family up here in the mountains, and one guy is dead. And for that matter, the family isn't any crazier than most families, mine included."

Back at the rockfall, Cal picked up his blankets, and then the two walked back towards the camp. The sunlight was slowly gaining a slight orange tint as the day grew towards evening, and the colors of the lake were even more vivid now than before. The green needles of the trees were now tinged with just a slight edge of gold, and the wind seemed to sense the changes, and softened its breath.

Dan looked at the blankets and said to Cal, "You still have time to make it down the trailhead before it gets dark."

"I know, but I'll be fine. Right now I want to talk to the rest of these people and try to put together a few more pieces on this thing."

"I've talked to Peter and Luke," Dan said. "And also Kristen."

"And don't forget our boy Rafael," Cal added.

"Yeah. So we still haven't talked to Veronica, and she was the one who found the body."

"And she was right along here somewhere when it happened," Cal reminded him,

"Yep," Dan agreed. And there are still two others. I met Gabriela. She's a piece of work. And there is one more sister here, too. I haven't seen her at all."

The two men picked their way across the stones in the outlet stream, hopping from one to the next. Once on the other side, they could see that the campfire had been re-kindled, and a group of people were clustered around it.

Dan pointed out Luke, standing next to Kristen. "The tall guy with the blond hair, that's Luke." He wondered why they seemed to be standing next to each other so often.

Peter sat on a log, sipping something in a mug. Gabriela was in front of the fire, seemingly in charge of the conversation. Veronica was standing with her back to them, next to another large woman dressed in a pastel yellow sweater. She looked just a bit like a large pale yellow easter egg.

"The one in yellow must be the other sister," Dan said.

"That's a lot of weight to lug up the trail," Cal replied.

The group around the campfire suddenly turned its attention to the two approaching men.

Gabriela walked through the group to meet them. "Where do we stand with all of this?" she asked them. "What's going on?"

Dan explained that they had found Rafael, who was fishing on the other side of the lake. And he explained that he and Cal were trying to put everything together so that they could write a report.

"What do you need to put together?" Gabriela asked. "Peter accidentally knocked a rock off the cliff, and it fell down and hit our father. That seems pretty clear." Her face was now quite close to Dan's, looking up into his eyes. Dan was glad that his sunglasses gave him a little protection from her invasion of his space.

It was Cal who spoke next. "We are just trying to make sure that we don't make any mistakes," he said. "We know your father was an important man, and lots of people are going to ask questions. We just want to make sure that when they do, we have the answers." He paused, then looked right at Gabriela. "I'm sure that's what you'd want us to do."

Dan had to admit that Cal was pretty good at defusing the situation. Gabriela turned back towards her family and spoke to them. "What is it you need from us?"

Cal again stepped forward. "Okay, what we usually like to do is talk to each person individually, just to get all the various facts. That lets us put it all in order, and we can write it up."

He nodded his head in the direction of Dan and continued. "I know Ranger Courtwright has spoken to Peter and Luke and Kristen. And we've also been able to talk to Rafael. So if you would be willing to give us a few minutes, we'd like to talk to the rest of you as well."

"Do you really think we're going to tell you anything you don't already know?" Gabriela asked.

Dan nodded. "Rafael saw someone around on the rocks below the cliff this morning. That's something we didn't know before." He turned to Peter. "Did you notice anyone, Peter?"

Peter looked up blankly, almost stunned. "No, I didn't see anyone… I don't think." He shook his head as if to emphasize his answer.

Gabriela took a quick glance around, then said, "Fine. Gloria, if you can leave those crackers alone for a minute, why don't you go first?"

Gloria's eyes flickered in anger, or was it embarrassment? But she didn't argue. "And then Veronica… and that leaves me for last." She turned with a questioning look, confronting the two men, as if daring them to disagree.

"Okay…" Cal grudgingly accepted her schedule.

Dan wasn't pleased with the way Gabriela had taken charge of the process. And he didn't like the idea that while he and Cal were talking to Gloria, Gabriela might spend some time trying to prepare Veronica for her interview. "Actually," he said in a conciliatory tone, "we don't need for this to go on all evening. There are two of us, so we can each talk to someone. Cal?" he turned to the Sheriff, "Would you like to chat with Veronica, while I talk to Gloria?"

"Sure," Dan replied. "Gloria, why don't you and I walk over to the lake, so we don't get interrupted?"

Dan looked around a saw a log resting among a few rocks about fifty yards away, surrounded by a few young fir trees. He suggested to Veronica that they have a seat on the log, and the two of them slowly walked there.

Veronica brushed off the log briefly, then carefully sat down. She sat, almost posed, with her hands on her knees, feet together, looking out over the lake. As Dan watched her, she took a big breath and slumped her shoulders a bit. She looked even smaller as she sat there.

Dan waited a moment. He could see her hands trembling slightly as she pressed them to her knees, and he noticed that her feet were making small movements, as if trying to slowly burrow into the powdery dirt. Tiny ridges of the dirt began to form around her hiking shoes.

Dan began in a very gentle voice. "What can you tell about all of this?" he asked. But he was unprepared for the answer he got.

"I'm not like the other people in this family," Veronica said. "They're all really successful... they have big jobs and amazing skills... I don't have any of that."

Dan had no idea where this was going, but he didn't want to interrupt.

"I'm just a mom," Veronica continued. "They all have their businesses, and they're always traveling all over the place. And I stay at home and take care of my kids. I don't have a fancy car, or a big house. I don't have any special skills. Sometimes I am not even sure I'm related to them. And they don't treat me like I am, either."

There was an edge of disappointment in her voice.

Dan saw an opportunity to learn more and didn't want to let it pass. "So when you were growing up...?" He let the question dangle.

"They were always busy with stuff," Veronica remembered. "My dad always made sure that we each had our special activities. You can see it now, in how they are. Everybody but me. Peter climbs—he's world famous for that. And he's a great athlete. Gloria writes about food and wine for big magazines, and she has her own line of foods she sells. Gabriela runs the business. She is so smart. Rafael is just driven. He has so much energy... he hates to slow down..."

She let the conversation drift to a stop.

Dan pretended to be writing notes, but was really just allowing Veronica to continue at her own pace. Maybe she needed a nudge. "Don't you have another sister?"

Veronica nodded. "Sophie. We're twins. She's an artist. She does pottery and painting, all sorts of stuff. When we were growing up she was always the one to get dirty, and I was the one to clean her up. Her paintings are beautiful."

"And she is not here this week, is that right?" Dan asked.

Veronica shook her head. "She refuses to play the game. For a long time I managed to convince her to come along, just to be part of the family, but for the past few years she has refused. She says it just isn't worth it to her any more even though it means that she won't get any of the estate."

Dan looked carefully at Veronica's face. "How does that work?" he asked.

For the first time Veronica looked at Dan. "That's the deal," she said. "If you join the family for the adventure, you get to share in the estate. If you don't come up here, you get cut off. Sophie doesn't care anymore." She looked away from Dan. "I guess that means more for the rest of us… as if we needed it."

Dan thought about this for a second. "Wow. This is more than just a family camping trip," he said. "This is kind of a command performance?"

Veronica nodded. "It was my dad's idea. He loved this area, and so he insisted that we hold the board meetings up here. And if you don't play along, if you don't attend, you don't get any of the money."

"Did that create any problems?" Dan asked.

"Only with Sophie. I mean… everybody has their complaints. Well… not Peter. He loves it here. But Gloria; this is not her cup of tea. And Luke would love to be somewhere else—almost anywhere else. I guess Gabriela is fine with it…."

"Luke seemed to enjoy his hike up the dome today," Dan offered.

"There must have been a woman on top," Veronica responded dryly, then immediately reconsidered. "I'm sorry. I shouldn't have said that."

Dan's mind began to drift to what that remark may have meant. Veronica noticed the pause and looked up at him.

Dan composed himself and looked back at his notepad. "So talk to me about today, Veronica. What happened?"

"I don't know. I heard Peter yelling and went to see what was going on. And then I saw Dad lying there on the ground…"

"Tell me about earlier in the morning. When did you get up? Talk me through your morning."

"I got up kind of late," she began. "Dad made sure we all got up before nine, like he always does." She looked at Dan, and he nodded. "I got up and got dressed. That takes me more time than the others. Luke was still in camp, pestering the cook. When Gloria and I got up, he left. We ate breakfast and then Dad made sure we all left camp."

Dan asked about Gabriela.

"I don't think Dad knows about it, knew about it," Veronica corrected herself, "but she has a little office in her tent. She always makes a big deal of getting up and getting going, but she's been working in her tent for a couple of hours, checking emails and things."

"Did she leave with the rest of you?" Dan asked.

"Yeah, more or less. You should ask her."

"Okay. So you finished breakfast…"

"Yes. And I wanted to just relax," Veronica continued. "I told Dad I was going to look for flowers, but I really just wanted to find a nice place by the lake and read a magazine. I never get to do that at home. I am too busy with the house and the kids."

"So you left camp when?" Dan pressed.

"I don't know. Whenever Dad told us we had to get going. Gloria was going to go look for some kind of mushroom on this side of the lake, and I went with Dad for a while. As soon as I saw a place to leave the trail and hide in the woods, I took it."

"And your dad? What did he do?" asked Dan.

"The last time I saw him, he was just walking up the trail. I wanted to make sure he didn't follow me, so I checked on him from the trees. He was walking up the trail, looking around at everything. He seemed really happy."

"And then?"

Veronica shrugged. "I found a comfy place to sit and opened up my magazines." She paused. "And then later I heard Peter yelling."

"Did you see anyone in the rocks with your father?" The ranger wanted to make sure he didn't miss any details that Veronica might have noted

"No, only Peter up on the cliff. He was hanging from a rope, sliding down towards Dad. Rappelling."

"Rafael said that he saw someone else over there, someone in camouflage clothes," Dan said. "Did you see that?"

"No," Veronica shook her head. "I didn't see anyone else."

"And did you see anything unusual around your dad? Did you see the rock that hit him? Anything that seemed odd?" Dan continued his questioning.

"What do you mean? He was there on the ground. There was a lot of blood. I didn't see the rock—but I didn't look for it, either. This seems mean, but I really didn't want to touch him. And I was sure he was dead." She looked up at Dan. "That's all there is, right?"

Dan watched her face as he asked her, "And you didn't touch anything else? You just waited for Peter to get down."

Veronica's face seemed to fog over a bit at this question, and she looked hard at Dan. "I didn't touch anything," she said. "Peter was there in a minute or so, screaming about how stupid he was, and how sorry he was."

Dan nodded.

And, Veronica added derisively, "That's the first time I've ever heard Peter say he was stupid!"

# chapter 10

Back at the camp, Cal was waiting for Dan by the fire. Gabriela and Gloria stood there with him, while the rest of the family had wandered off. Dan noticed Kristen come out of her tent and walk back over to the fire, adjusting her clothes as she walked. First she tucked her shirt into her shorts, then straightened the shorts themselves. Dan found himself wondering if she had been alone in her tent. As she got closer to the group, she mentioned that it was about time to get supper started.

They watched Veronica kneel down in front of her tent, peeling the zipper open, and then slowly climb inside, headfirst. The tent slowly swallowed her up, first head, then torso, then rear end, and finally just her feet stuck outside. One by one, they too wiggled inside. The tent moved for a few seconds; then one boot came flying out. The second soon followed and the tent shuddered, then was still.

Cal turned to Gabriela. "Would you talk to us for a few minutes?" he asked.

"Sure," she responded confidently. "Do you want to talk right here?"

Dan smiled. "Veronica and I found a really nice log over there that probably has room for three..." he offered.

"Okay, let's go there," Gabriela decided, and led the way.

Cal started the questioning by asking Gabriela what she had done that morning.

"I don't think that's any of your business," Gabriela replied.

Dan couldn't help thinking that this was not going to be fun. He stepped in and tried to smooth things over. "We just need to fill out our reports, and to do that, we need to explain where everyone was. When your father died, I mean."

"That makes no sense," said Gabriela. "He was killed by a rock that fell on the other side of the lake. It makes no difference where I was, or what I was doing. And I can't imagine why you would need that information for your report."

Cal took another tack. "Ms. Himmel, you are the manager of your father's businesses, isn't that right?"

Gabriela nodded. "I am the CEO of the parent corporation. The various companies report to me, and I report, reported, to my father."

Cal continued his line of reasoning. "Will you continue to run these companies, now that your father is gone?"

"Of course," Gabriela agreed. "Unless the board of directors removes me. But I don't think they will. I am the best one for the job."

Cal pressed on. "And as the CEO, do you want it to get out that you did not cooperate with the official investigation into your father's death?"

Gabriela seemed to take a minute to compose herself, and then responded. "I am perfectly happy to cooperate with you as you write your report on my father's death," she said firmly. "But I am not willing to divulge information to you that has nothing to do with his death. Where and how I spent this morning falls into that category."

This was met with silence from the two men. After a quick glance at Cal, Dan was the next to speak. "We have a problem right now," he said. "Nobody actually saw what happened to your father. And yet there were a lot of people around here. Veronica was on the other side of the lake, relatively close to your father, and she didn't see or hear anything until Peter started yelling. And nobody else saw or heard anything. So right now, we have to say that until we get more information, your father's death falls into the category of somewhat suspicious circumstances. And until we can eliminate all the variables, it will have to be announced that way."

Gabriela spoke slowly, as if to small children: "Peter said he knocked a rock off the cliff. It fell down and hit my father in the head. That seems tragic, maybe even stupid, but not suspicious." She stared at Dan, then at Cal. "Are you saying that Peter planned to hit my father with that rock? Because he was about five hundred feet straight up a cliff, and not even Peter is that good."

Cal allowed just a touch of frustration to creep into his voice as he responded. "Did you see that happen?" He waited, but then continued before Gabriela could formulate her answer. "Did Peter see the rock hit your father? Did Veronica see it? Was anyone else with your father when this happened? Were you?"

Before Gabriela could answer, Dan quietly suggested a few more questions. "Did you see anyone else up here, other than your family? We would really like to know that. And it would really help us to eliminate some variables if you could tell us where you were, and what you saw during the course of this morning."

Gabriela considered all the questions, then spoke quietly. "The only person here who is not part of our family is the cook. What's her name? Kristen. I think you know that. I left camp with my father and Veronica. When we got to the junction at the outlet stream, they walked up towards the lake, and I walked the other direction, over the ridge and towards the trailhead. I didn't see anyone or anything until the Search and Rescue team drove up, and that's when I came back over that ridge and learned about the accident and my father's death."

Cal was curious. "How far down the trail did you go once you got over the ridge? And did you leave the trail at any point? Would you have seen someone if they walked up the trail?"

"Nobody came up the trail this morning. If they had, I would have seen them. Just the ambulance crew."

Cal and Dan waited for the rest of the answer, but Gabriela stopped there.

"So how far down the trail did you go?" asked Dan. "Did you get all the way to the trailhead?"

Gabriela looked at him squarely in the face and said calmly, "I went all the way to the trailhead. I didn't leave the trail. I would have seen anyone who hiked up it this morning."

Cal jumped in at this point, and asked, "Why did you walk out? Did you meet someone there?"

"That has no bearing on your work, so I am not going to answer it," Gabriela said. "If you need any witnesses to where I was, you can certainly ask your rescue team. They saw me and can vouch for my whereabouts." A light breeze ruffled her hair, and Dan couldn't help thinking that was the only thing that was making her even a bit ruffled.

She suddenly stood up and turned to face the men. "I think that's all that I can offer you in terms of information," she said. "I hope you found it helpful. I am now going back to camp to be with the rest of my family. As you can imagine, this is a rather difficult time for us."

And with that she walked off, leaving the two men to watch her go.

"Well," said Cal with a slight drawl, "you can see why she's the one Dad picked to run the show, can't you?"

Dan nodded. "Hey, what did you find out from Gloria? I've got to say that Veronica has pretty much confirmed what we've heard already. Not much help there. Except that she must resent the rest of the family. According to her, everyone is better and more talented than she is."

"That must be depressing," Cal suggested. "Gloria wasn't much help, either. She didn't see anything. She had her nose buried in the ground, looking for mushrooms. From what she said, I guess she pretty much lives to eat and drink. Apparently, she's famous."

"For what?" Dan asked.

"She's a food expert, wine judge. She's been on TV. I guess that helps explain her weight."

The two stood for a minute, looking up at the cliff on the far side of the lake. As they turned to walk back to the camp, Dan said, "Why did Gabriela walk back out to the trailhead?"

Cal nodded. "Yeah. She mentioned the ambulance driving up. She must have been in the parking lot when they arrived, or she wouldn't have known it was an ambulance. I thought hiking out of here was against the rules."

"Maybe Gabriela doesn't have to follow the rules," Dan suggested. "After all, she's the boss."

"Or maybe she does, and she doesn't want anyone to know that she broke them," Cal said. "So who did she meet?"

Dan agreed. "She had to be meeting someone. Is there any chance the SAR team saw who it was?"

Cal pulled his radio out and called Sara, quickly outlining what he wanted to know. Sara promised that she would ask the crew and get back to him. As he put the radio back in its holster, he asked Dan, "So what do you think is for dinner?"

Dan laughed. "I hope Kristen has something for us to eat. Because if she doesn't, I'm down to my last couple of energy bars."

Cal snorted. "Shit! I thought you guys were supposed to be prepared for anything!"

"That's the Boy Scouts," Dan laughed. "But you won't die if you miss a meal or two."

"I am not missing a meal, at least not this one," Cal responded. "Hell, if we have to, we are going to confiscate those trout we saw and eat them!"

# chapter 11

Back at the camp, Dan noted that Kristen was stirring a couple of different pots over a two-burner stove, and walked over to ask her if she wanted any help.

"I think I have the food under control," she said. "But if you really want to help, you could get the dishes out of that blue box over there." She stopped to look at Dan for a moment. "Are you guys joining us for dinner?"

With an embarrassed smile, Dan asked, "If that's okay? Do you have enough food?"

"Oh, yeah," Kristen reassured him. "We have plenty of food, if you are willing to eat what we have…"

"I'm sure it tastes better than the two energy bars I have left in my pack," Dan said with a chuckle. "And I'm impressed. I've been living off freeze-dried dinners for the last week. This looks pretty good, and smells good, too."

"I put together the menu in advance, so I can put it together pretty quickly once we're here," Kristen explained. "And they give me a mule to carry the food in on the first day. Since weight isn't much of an issue, I can add a few treats to make things more interesting."

"So what are we having?" Dan couldn't help but lean in and try to see what was cooking in the pot.

"You can't tell?" Kristen teased him. Before he could react, she added, "It's macaroni and cheese. I've got some pea soup in this pot," she said pointing to the one on the left.

Kristen paused to look around the campsite. "So you are spending the night here?" she asked.

Dan nodded. "We decided that it was better to try and get all this done today..."

Kristen pulled her spoon out of one of the pots and looked at Dan. "What exactly are you getting done?" she asked.

Much as he wanted to, Dan realized that he could not explain his suspicions to Kristen. He sighed. "You wouldn't believe the kinds of reports we have to fill out when something like this happens," he said. "It's just a lot of questions and a lot of paperwork."

As they chatted, Veronica and Gloria walked out of the trees to the north of the campsite and joined them around the campfire ring. Cal wandered in and asked Dan where he was going to pitch his tent. Dan looked around at the options, then hefted up his pack and pointed to an area up the hill from the camp. "If we can find a flat spot up there, I think that might work," he said.

As the two men walked past one of the nearby tents, they could hear Gabriela talking to someone in her tent. They exchanged a glance and kept walking, up beyond the trail. Dan found a small clearing and put his pack down.

"You're camping here?" Cal asked. "Why?"

"I want to give them a little space," Dan answered. "That's their camp. This can be ours."

Cal disagreed. "If we were just backpacking, I'd agree," he said, "but I want to be closer to them. I want to hear what people say for as long as they are saying it."

Dan thought about this. He really didn't want to pick his pack back up and carry it back to the camp, but he had to admit that Cal had a point.

Cal indicated the backpack and asked, "What kind of a tent do you have in there?"

"It's just a tarp." Dan explained. "It keeps the rain off, but that's about it. But there is room for you, if you want to..."

Cal looked back at the larger campsite. "You know where I want to sleep?" he asked Dan. "I want to be over by those big rocks on the far side of their camp. We won't be right on top of them, but I bet those rocks help us hear what's going on."

Instead of waiting for Dan's answer, Cal picked up the ranger's pack and started to carry over to the rocks. As they walked through the Himmels' camp, he smiled at the women around the fire pit and explained, "Change of plans. I sleep better with a real headboard."

Once by the rocks, Dan opened up the pack and unloaded his tarp and ground cover. Cal was observing the family members. "So we've got Veronica and Gloria there by Kristen, and Gabriela is in her tent. Where are the guys?"

Dan shook his head to show that he didn't know the answer to the question. He took a break from setting up the tarp to look around. "I don't know. In their tents? Off in the woods somewhere?"

"And more important," Cal continued, interrupting Dan, "what do you think is for dinner?"

Dan smiled. "Mac and cheese. Soup. She's probably got some crackers there, too, and some cookies or something for dessert. They pack it in on a mule."

"I was wondering how that heavy gal was going to carry a pack with all her stuff in it up here," Cal said. "She's carrying a lot of weight as it is."

"She made it up here. That's more than most people do," said Dan. He was pulling the lines taut on the tarp, stretching it out into a flat panel, angled downwards towards the lake. "I give her credit for that."

"That's your tent?" Cal asked incredulously. "Where's the rest of it?"

Dan smiled. "If you had to carry this pack for a week, you'd be very happy with this thing," he said. "It keeps me dry, and that's all I ask."

"Hmmph," Cal snorted. "I thought you'd offer me better accommodations."

"I would," Dan replied, "but the lodge was fully booked tonight. You get to enjoy the outdoors."

Dan finished tossing his sleeping pad and bag under the tarp, making sure to fluff up the sleeping bag just a bit as he did so. Then he turned to Cal. "I'm done here. Let's go get your blankets and toss them over here so we don't have to find our way around in the dark."

Walking back to the fire pit, Dan heard Cal's radio crackle. Cal stopped and turned around, walking back towards their tent as he listened. Dan was tempted to follow him, but out of the corner of his eye he caught someone walking back from the lake. It was Peter, wearing only a bathing suit, with a towel draped over his shoulder. Dan decided to walk back to the camp and join the conversation there. Cal would bring him up to speed on his radio conversation, but Dan wanted to hear what the rest of the family had to say to each other.

Peter was a different man, now that he was clean. You could see it even in the way he walked back into the camp. There was an awkward moment as he arrived; then Gloria went up to him and put her arms around him. Veronica stood nearby, then reached out one arm and patted Peter on the shoulder as well.

It was Kristen who broke up the support group, as she announced that dinner was ready. Veronica walked over to her tent and called to Gabriela to join the group for dinner. Gloria was carefully laying out the plates and helping Kristen serve, while Peter sat down on a log and began rubbing his short hair with the towel.

In just a few minutes they were all sitting on the same log, each with a cup of soup and a bowl of macaroni in front of them. Dan chose a spot on another log nearby, and then explained to Kristen that Cal would arrive at any minute—he was just finishing up a radio call.

When Gabriela came out of her tent, she looked surprised to see Dan sitting with the rest of the family. "Oh, I see you are joining us for dinner?" There was a tart note in her voice that made it clear she hoped that Dan wouldn't stay long.

"I invited them," Kristen explained. "We had plenty of food, and I didn't want it to go to waste. And up here, there is no such thing as leftovers. We can use the help tonight."

Gabriela wasn't happy, but she wasn't going to admit it. "No, that's fine, Kristen. I agree."

Kristen stood over the pots, with a few bowls still waiting to be filled. "Where are Luke and Rafael?" she asked.

Dan pointed over to where he had set his tarp. "Cal is right there. He'll be here in a minute. If you want to serve his food, I'll keep an eye on it until he gets here."

"No, I don't want it to get cold. It will stay warmer in the pot," Kristen insisted. "So where are the other two?"

"Rafael will be late," Gabriela said. "He's fishing, and we won't see him until it is too dark for him to see the lake." She paused, looking around. "I don't know where Luke is…"

Dan saw Cal put his radio back in the holster and start walking towards the fire pit.

"Are you ready for your dinner?" Kristen called out to him.

"Sounds great!" Cal responded. As Kristen filled his hands with a cup, bowl, spoon, and crackers, he remarked, "And it looks great, too! Thanks for all of this…"

Gabriela turned to Peter. "How are you doing, Peter?"

Peter shrugged, chewing his food, then looked down at the ground. He finally swallowed and said "It's been a tough day. I'll be glad to get in my bag and go to sleep tonight."

Cal sat down next to Dan on the second log and held his bowl up in front of his face. He quietly whispered to Dan, "That was Sara on the radio."

Dan waited for Cal to continue. Both men stared off in the distance as they spoke, in the hopes that their conversation wouldn't draw the attention of the others around the fire pit. "I figured," Dan said.

"The SAR team saw Gabriela at the trailhead," Cal said. Another pause, followed by another spoonful of macaroni. Then he called out, "This is really good mac and cheese, Kristen."

A murmur of agreement rose out of the group.

Cal turned back to Dan. "She was there when they arrived, just like we thought. And guess who else was there?"

Dan looked at him and shrugged.

Cal continued, "Sophie Himmel."

"Is that the other sister?" Dan asked.

Cal nodded. "Sara is good. The SAR team just about got run off the road by a car on their way to the trailhead. They called it in and gave her a description, and one of our officers met the car when it arrived in Tuolumne City. She was still speeding, so they gave her a ticket."

Dan pondered this while they ate. He looked up to see Luke arrive in camp, walking up the trail from the lake. Most of the lake was in shadow now, and only the granite cliffs above it were still in sun, a dull, orange sunlight.

Cal looked at Dan. "It kinda makes you wonder what Sophie was doing there, huh?"

Dan agreed. "And why she was in such a hurry to leave."

Cal stared at the top of Clark Dome, just visible high above the trees from where they sat. "I don't know what the hell happened up here today, but we are going to figure this out," he said.

After dinner, Dan and Cal offered to take care of cleaning up. "It's the least we can do to pay for dinner," Dan said. Kristen tried to explain that it was actually part of her job, but Dan and Cal were already on their way down to the lake to bring back a couple of pots of water.

When they got back to camp, Kristen had lit a small fire in the fire pit, and the family was gathered around it. The two men quickly washed the dishes and helped Kristen put the food away so that everything was set for the night.

The conversation was subdued. Luke mentioned that their father would have enjoyed the dinner, and the time around the campfire with the rest of the family.

"Well," Gloria said, "we're here because of him. I don't think any of us would be here on our own."

"Peter would," Luke suggested. "He'd rather be here than anywhere else in the world!"

"Yeah, I would," Peter agreed. "I love these mountains."

"Oh, I like the mountains, too," said Veronica. "I just wish that we didn't have to hike here, or sleep on the ground."

As they sat on logs around the fire, the warmth of the fire drew them together. The glow lit their faces as the sky turned first pink, then violet overhead. A single star, Vega, appeared between the trees above them, and within a few minutes more stars were visible. In the west a pale pink glow backlit the trees, and then it was night.

Dan and Cal decided to turn in early. They still hoped to spend some time talking about the events of the day, and they wanted to do that in private. Dan walked into the woods to heed a call of nature, while Cal walked to their tent.

From over his shoulder Dan heard Cal mutter an obscenity under his breath, then in a louder voice, call out, "Hey, Dan?"

Dan turned around and walked towards the tent. Cal was kneeling in front of it, with his flashlight aimed inside. The Sheriff was frozen in place.

Dan's flesh turned to goose bumps as he crept up to Cal. "What's going on?" he asked.

Cal's flashlight shone into the tarp, aimed at Dan's sleeping bag. "What the fuck is that?" he said quietly, his voice tense.

Dan could now see underneath the tarp, where his sleeping bag was lying. But there was something odd about it. He remembered making sure to fluff the bag up, to shake the down loose. But the bag wasn't lying flat. In fact, there was somebody inside it.

Or, Dan thought with a shudder of fear, there was a body in his sleeping bag.

# chapter 12

Dan stared at his sleeping bag. There was something odd about the way the bag looked, with some unusual bulges around the chest and arms. He stared hard, trying to detect any motion.

When he looked at Cal, he saw the Sheriff looking back over his shoulder at the campfire. "I'm just counting," Cal whispered. "I was trying to see if anyone is missing, but they're all there, except Rafael… and I don't see Kristen."

Dan looked to see the group now sitting around the glowing embers of the campfire. He could see light reflecting off the glasses of Luke, and Peter sat tall in the middle. The three Himmel women sat together on one side, leaning against each other. He turned to look at Kristen's tent, and saw a light glowing inside. He pointed with his chin. "That's Kristen over there." As they watched, her light flashed on the side of the tent, then back on the roof. Maybe she was reading.

Cal turned back to their own tent and reached out and nudged the foot in the sleeping bag. "Hey. Wake up," he said quietly. There was no response, but Cal reacted with a snort. He shoved the bag hard and the bag shot across the floor of the tarp, hitting the far side. Cal leaped under the tarp and yanked the sleeping bag open. A head and face appeared, but even in the light of their flashlights Dan could see that that there was something odd about it. Then the plastic arms appeared.

"It's a fucking inflatable doll," Cal said angrily, ripping it out of the bag and throwing it out from under the tarp. "Very funny." He shined his light into Dan's face, expecting to see a grin, but Dan was stunned, his expression mimicking the frozen expression on the doll's face.

He turned and looked at the campfire. From here it looked as if Peter was now sitting next to Luke, and the two men were facing the ranger's tarp. "Very funny," Dan said quietly, still looking at the two men by the fire.

Cal lifted the doll out from under the tarp and held it in one hand. "I'm going to take this over to them…" he paused as he thought through his next move.

"Don't make a big deal out of it, Cal," Dan said. "Just hand it to them and let's get some sleep."

"Are you kidding?" Cal asked incredulously. "I'm going to find out whose idea this was, and then I'm going to toss this thing on the fire, and then I'm going handcuff a couple of them and make them sweat!"

"Well, my guess is that this is Luke's idea of a joke," Dan said. "And my guess is that the others may not even know he did it. So if you go after all of them, they're all going to get angry. If you downplay the whole thing, I bet the others will take our side instead of his. And maybe we can use that. At least it would be better than having them all angry."

Cal thought about this for a minute, then agreed. "Okay. Why Luke?" he asked.

"Something one of the others said about Luke… something about his, uh, interest in sex."

"Asshole," Cal said.

"Yeah," Dan agreed.

"Jesus, people are so stupid," Cal said.

"Yeah," Dan agreed again. He could see that Cal was calming down, and that was a good thing. Now that the adrenaline was disappearing, Dan felt better as well.

Cal slowly started walking towards the campfire. Dan sat back and started unlacing his boots for the first time all day. As his fingers struggled with the dusty knots, he called out quietly, "Hey Cal, you also don't want to toss that thing on the fire. Makes a horrible smell, and it won't really burn right. Make them pack it out... and we'll make sure they do."

Cal looked back over his shoulder at Dan, nodded, and then walked over to the campfire. From where Dan was sitting, he could see the family begin to react. The three girls sat up, and soon he could hear their voices raised, yelling at Luke. Peter stared at the ground. Luke seemed to raise his cup as a kind of salute to Cal, and as Dan watched Cal tossed the doll right at Luke, making him spill whatever was in his cup. He heard Gabriela say, "Serves you right."

Dan had pulled off his boots and then lay back onto the sleeping bag. He could still see the campfire group, but his body was luxuriating in the soft down and the flat surface of his camp. He let out a small groan of pleasure, then slowly turned slightly on his side so that he could see Cal.

Cal finished talking to the family, turned, and started to walk back towards Dan, when he paused and turned to face the group again. Dan could not hear what was being said, but it was clearly a serious conversation. He saw the heads around the campfire slowly shaking back and forth, saying no. After only a few minutes, Cal walked back to Dan.

"I hope you're not getting into that sleeping bag," he said to Dan. "We've got a small problem."

"What's that?" Dan asked.

"Our fishing buddy has gone missing. Nobody's seen him since we talked to him this afternoon. And they say that he is always back before dark."

"He didn't ever come back for dinner?" Dan asked.

"Nope. Nobody's seen him. If that SOB has taken off, I am going to be really pissed."

Dan let out a big sigh and sat up. "Does that mean we have to go looking for him?"

"I'm going to radio in to have someone drive up to the trailhead and check on the cars there… but they are going to ask me where he was last seen. And I think we ought to go back there and see if we can find him. Just to make sure he didn't sprain an ankle and is sitting in the middle of the trail somewhere."

Dan groaned as reached out for his boots and started pulling them back on his feet. They seemed tighter now than they had been only five minutes before.

"Do you have a good light?" Cal asked him.

"Yeah… and I am sure they have more over in their camp," Dan replied. "How do you want to do this?"

Cal thought this over, then explained to Dan, "If he was fishing at the top of the lake, he could have tried to come back to camp either way, on this side or the other side of the lake." He said, "Why don't I go up the far side, and you work your way up this side. And we'll try to meet more or less where we saw him last, up on the creek. Does that make sense?"

"And do we just leave these people here?" Dan asked.

"I am not sure I trust these people to help me," Cal answered him. "Do you want to take some of them with you?"

Dan thought about this. "It always helps to have more eyes and ears," he said, "but I am not sure how much help they would be."

The two men were startled by a noise behind them.

"Hi, guys. What's going on?" Kristen asked.

Dan explained the situation to Kristen, while Cal got on his radio back to Sonora.

"Did Rafael say anything about staying out late, or missing dinner?" Dan asked Kristen.

"No, he fished until about dark, but he usually fished his way back towards camp as it got dark... so he was never very late," Kristen answered. "Did he eat the food I left for him?"

Cal looked up from his radio and said "Nope... food's still there."

"Do you want some help looking for him?" Kristen asked.

Dan felt more gratitude than he expected at this offer. He was surprised at the sudden warmth in his chest. "Sure, that would be great," he replied. "We were just saying that more eyes are better and trying to decide if we should ask some of the family to help."

"I'm sure they'd be happy to do it," Kristen said. "At least Peter and Luke... and Gabriela. I'm not sure about the others."

"We were going to break up into two groups and go up each side of the lake," Dan explained to Kristen. "Do you know your way around? Do you have a preference which side you'd like to take?"

There was an awkward pause, then Kristen said firmly, "Whichever side Luke is not on."

Cal put away his radio and said, "Okay—then you two take this side of the lake, and I'll ask the others to join me on the other side. Does that sound good?"

# chapter 13

While Cal walked back over to the campfire to organize the rest of the family, Dan and Kristen slowly found their way down to the trail around the lake. It was dark enough that they could clearly see stars, but the quarter moon overhead added enough light to cast a shadow under the trees. Dan wore his headlamp, a tiny light that cast a focused circular beam in front him. Kristen had a small handheld flashlight that she left off most of the time, allowing Dan's light to illuminate the path in front of them.

There was no official trail on the west side of the lake, but over the years, fishermen had worn a clear path along the edge. Dan followed this path along, and where the path got close to the lake, he stopped to look along the shore.

It was slow progress, but the night was silent, and the reflection of the moon overhead lit the water as if through a murky lens. Across the lake, the solid white monolith of the Monument almost glowed in the moonlight, showing long, weeping traces of black streaming down the face.

Halfway up the lakeshore, the path crossed a small feeder stream, and Dan carefully picked his way across on top of a few large stones. He then turned and pointed his light at the rocks, to show Kristen the way. As she hopped across the rocks he held out his hand, and helped her up the side of the creek. He wasn't sure if it was the right thing to do.

"Thanks," she said, but to his disappointment she quickly removed her hand from his.

They followed the path another few feet until they reached the top of a small rise on the west side of the lake. Here a rockfall from the hill behind had nearly reached the lake, and the path wound itself up, around and through the boulders. At the top of the rocks, they could see the whole lake beneath them. In the moonlight the shoreline was still visible, curving around the north end of the lake, and finally disappearing in a grove of trees where the stream entered at the head of the lake. A small island stood offshore, with just a few trees and rocks above the water's surface.

"Look!" Kristen called to him. "You can see the others on the far side."

Dan saw the lights from flashlights along the far shore. The other group had farther to go and was well behind them on their trip to the north end of the lake. Their lights were blinking and wandering, and Dan was grateful he wasn't with that group.

He stood on the rocks and watched the flashes of light from the other side. It was very quiet. Dan could hear Kristen breathing next to him, and a soft whisper of breeze through the trees at the north end of the lake. The temperature was cooling off, but Dan realized that the rocks were radiating heat they had collected during the day, creating a perfect balance to the breeze.

"We're going to get there ahead of them," he said to Kristen. He could feel her standing close, even sense the warmth of her body.

Kristen was staring at the Monument. "It's like snow," she said. "So white. And the lake is so black."

Dan sighed. "I don't think we're going to find this guy," he said. He continued to look down the shore, but there was no motion or light on their side of the lake. "I think he may have hiked out of here."

"Why do you say that?" Kristen asked.

Dan knew that he shouldn't tell Kristen his suspicions. "I think he may have just decided to get the hell out of here," he said.

"Well… that would surprise me," Kristen said.

It was Dan's turn to ask the question. "Why do you say that?"

"Oh, just from the discussions they had over the last couple of days," Kristen said. "I don't think that Rafael got what he wanted, and I don't think that he was ready to leave here until he did."

"What do you mean?" asked Dan. "What did he want?"

"You know that this family runs a lot of businesses, right?" Kristen asked. "Well, the last couple of days, after dinner, they would have their meetings to discuss their businesses. They all have to make reports and then request any changes or actions from the rest of the family."

Dan sat down on one of the rocks and invited Kristen to do the same. She chose a rock a few feet away and continued her explanation. "He really wanted some things to change, and tonight was the night they were going to make all the final decisions for next year." She paused. "I just think that he wouldn't leave here without finding out if he was going to get what he asked for."

"What was that?" Dan asked.

"Do you know what each of them does?" Kristen asked Dan.

"I just know they all run different parts of the family business," he said. "How do you know all of this?"

Kristen laughed softly. "They hire me because I don't have a television, and don't get a newspaper," she said. "Because this whole thing is really a board meeting for the family business. And I am there for the whole thing, either cooking or cleaning up. They've hired me for the last four years, and part of the agreement is that I am going to hear things, and I am not supposed to repeat them." She paused. "But now that Max is dead, I think that changes things."

"So what did Rafael do?" Dan asked.

"He lives in Hungary," she answered. "They have a wine barrel company there, and he is in charge of it. And this year he was really insistent that they had to invest in some new equipment, or he wouldn't be able to compete. It's something about measuring or studying the wood for the barrels so that every barrel tastes exactly the same way."

"And do you think they were going to let him do that?" Dan asked.

"From what I heard, everybody had a story like that, and there wasn't enough money to go around," Kristen said. "All the others tried to make it sound like his problem wasn't as serious as theirs. But that's his big issue. He's also a huge soccer fan, and bought a team over there, which has lost millions of dollars. He even tried to sell the barrel company to raise more funds for the soccer team. That got squashed last year."

"That must have pissed him off," Dan suggested.

In the moonlight, Dan could see Kristen turn her head away from him, towards the lights on the other side of the lake. "He was furious. Those meetings are really hard," she said. "Max… Max was really tough, always making each person justify himself. And the others always jumped in, if they thought it would help their cause. This year was even worse—I guess because of the economy. But Max was furious that they were losing money, and he really cracked the whip on everyone. Nobody was happy."

"I'm glad my dad didn't have a business to inherit," Dan confessed.

"Yeah, but these are huge companies," Kristen said. "They're talking about multi-millions of dollars in each one, sometimes a hundred million or more. And the only one who seems to get what she wants is Gabriela."

"Why is that?" Dan asked.

"She's the CEO of the parent company," Kristen answered, "and she really knows how to play the game. She is the one person who can convince Max of anything at all. At least since his wife died."

Dan looked away from the lake and back at Kristen. "When was that?" he asked.

"About four years ago," she replied. "Christiana. She was a smoker, and she died from lung cancer. When that happened, the meetings got a lot angrier. She kind of held things together when she was here."

"And now?" Dan asked.

"Now it's ugly," Kristen said. "Everybody has a plan, and it's every man for himself. Except Veronica. She doesn't really want to be here. She just wants her share of the money so she can buy stuff. Clothes, mainly. And she's convinced that she's not getting it. That's why she comes—to make sure the others aren't cheating her."

"And Gloria?" Dan asked.

"Gloria lives to eat and drink. And she has the bad luck to have to come here and eat my food every year," Kristen said wryly.

"It tasted good to me," Dan assured her.

"Oh, it's fine, but she lives in New York, and knows every great restaurant everywhere in the world. So she's a little harder to please."

"What does she do, just eat and drink?" Dan asked.

"No," Kristen laughed. "They have a company that makes wine glasses and tableware. Gloria makes sure that every great restaurant in the world uses their products."

"Wow!" Dan exclaimed. "That must be fun work."

"That's exactly what the others say," Kristen replied. "They think that she spends too much money on that kind of thing. And she tells them that it's absolutely necessary. And she may be right. Her company always seems to make a good profit. Even this year."

Dan thought this over for a minute. "I'll bet that made Max happy, and proud," he said.

"Oh, God," Kristen muttered. "He always told her that anyone could make money with that company, because he had assembled such a good team there that any idiot could be successful. He was always after her to be more forceful. He thought they should dominate the market, and she wasn't strong enough to do that. She hated that. She told him to his face that it made her feel as if he didn't value her at all."

"Ouch," Dan said quietly.

"In some ways he felt that way about all the kids, I think," Kristen said. "It must have been really hard on them. He was always so much nicer to me than he was to any of them…"

"What does Luke do?" Dan asked. Kristen had apparently decided to share as much information as Dan wanted, and he couldn't resist trying to find out more about the Himmels and their businesses.

"Well, that's a big issue right now," she said. "Peter was down in Chile, way south in the mountains, running their lumber operations down there. And basically, not making any money, but spending a lot of time running a climbing and guide business down there instead. And then Luke apparently got into some kind of trouble, so he was sent down there to run that. Peter was furious. He was screaming about it."

"What kind of trouble?" asked Dan.

Kristen answered tightly, "He doesn't seem to be able to keep his hands off women. And a young woman in Switzerland finally decided to go after him for it. She sued him and the company, and it was pretty ugly. That was a couple of years ago. Luke got sent to Chile, and took Peter's place down there."

"Did that solve the problem?" Dan asked.

"Not really. Now Luke spends a lot of time traveling to Brazil on business, but everyone says it's just to meet women. They're just waiting for the next lawsuit. And Peter really lost his dream down in Chile. He was trying to manage the whole thing environmentally, and also have some kind of a climbing and adventure sport resort on the property. It never made any money when he was running it. Now Luke has really turned it around, but Peter swears he's ruining the land forever."

Dan found himself disliking Luke even more. "So what does Peter do now?" he asked.

"He was given a small loan to start a climbing and backpacking company here in California," Kristen said. "Max said that if he could make it profitable here, then they'd reconsider what was happening in Chile. But in the meantime, Peter swore Luke was ruining the property… and Peter doesn't make any money at all with his company. It's a total loss, a financial disaster. It's too easy for people to come here and hike and climb any time they want. They don't need his help to do that. So Max told him that it was over—that he had to go back to New York and work in the office there."

"And he didn't like that?" Dan asked.

"No—but nobody liked what Max was telling them," Kristen explained. "Nobody was happy this morning."

Dan could see the flashlights of the others were now across the lake from them. "If we are going to meet the others, we should get moving again." He stood up, and Kristen did the same, carefully keeping space between them. Dan would have welcomed an opportunity to get closer, but he was wary of making her uncomfortable. "Thank you for helping with this," he said to her. He felt the need to explain a bit more. "I guess we think that there may be more to this whole thing than we first thought, and we're just trying to figure it out."

"I know," she said. "You think maybe it wasn't an accident."

She wasn't asking Dan a question; she was making a statement. Dan saw no reason to correct her. As he turned to walk along the path up to meet the others, he said over his shoulder, "We're just trying to figure out what happened."

# chapter 14

During their conversation, Dan had turned off his headlamp, both to save batteries and to avoid shining the light into Kristen's eyes when he looked at her. As he looked down the path, he realized that the moonlight was enough for him to see where he was going.

"I think we can see well enough by the moonlight," he said to Kristen. He loved to walk in the mountains by moonlight. At this elevation the moon was like a beacon, and Dan could clearly see his shadow on the ground in front of him.

"Are you sure?" She sounded less confident than he was.

"The moon's pretty bright, and at least until we get into the trees, we should be able to follow the trail," he said. Dan began to walk gingerly down the trail. The moonlight was bright, but it did make him feel as if he had less depth perception. His eyes were seeing clearly, but his mind had a more difficult time interpreting the information.

To his right he could see the blinking and flickering lights of the other group as they began to work their way through the rocks where Max's body had been found. He was glad that he was not with them. In his mind he could still see clearly the black spot on the trail where Max's blood had stained the ground, and he could only imagine the impact that would have on the family as they passed by.

The northeast corner of the lake was a large flat meadow. It was a bog in the spring; the snowfields above it slowly melted into the grass and made it completely impassable. But by now, Dan thought they would be able to follow the trail along the lake shore. He was sure that was what Rafael would have done, being a fisherman. The trail dipped down between two boulders, and then they were walking along the edge of the rocks, with the huge meadow in front of them. The trail slowly wound around to the right until it reached the lake. When it reached the shore, there was a narrow track that carefully found its way north between the lake itself and the field of grass.

Here the trail was damp, and in places almost muddy. The mud was a rich black color, but where the water had washed over it, there were flecks of white granite that shone in the moonlight. Occasionally one would catch the light just right on a fractured face of quartz, and it sparkled against the black soil.

From time to time they came upon a log, bleached white over time, that had washed up along the shore. Twice these logs lay across their path, and they had to climb up and over them to continue. Others lay with one end on the shore, the other end deeply submerged under the black water of the lake. Dan knew that these were prime fishing spots, and he took extra care to look for any hint that Rafael had been there. But the footprints in the mud were old, and the mud was now dry enough that their own feet left almost no mark at all.

At the boggiest place on the trail, where the meadow drained into the lake, someone had dragged a log over to the trail to serve as a bridge across the muddiest spot. Dan thought about stepping up onto the log, then decided that he would test the mud first. His first few steps were met with firm ground underneath, and he gained confidence.

Kristen, walking behind, asked, "Are you sure this isn't going to be muddy?"

Dan smiled to himself. "I'm not sure," he answered, "but so far, so good."

His steps now were very careful, as he eased each foot into the mud. It was getting softer with each step, and he could see some standing water on the trail ahead. He kept to the left on the trail, trying to set his feet on the tufts of grass that stood slightly higher than the trail itself. And then, with one footstep, he sank four or five inches into the mud. With a leap he tried to extricate himself, sloshing and floundering for ten feet before he found solid ground again.

When he did, he turned around to look at Kristen. "You might want to try something different there," he said to her.

But Kristen had already turned on her flashlight. She calmly sat down on the log next to the trail and swung her feet up onto it as well. Arms out from her sides, she slowly stood up, still holding the flashlight in one hand, and began to balance her way down the log. When she reached Dan, she looked down at him and asked, "Is it dry there?"

"Yeah," he nodded and held out his hand to her.

She ignored it and walked past him on the log, then hopped down on the trail. She turned to him and waited for him to take the lead again.

Dan waved her forward, encouraging her to go first. "Go ahead," he said.

"No, you're doing great," she replied, standing back from the trail to let him go first.

Dan couldn't decide if he was flattered or being played for a fool. And he found himself thinking that either way, he didn't mind.

The trees at the head of the lake were the other primary campsite at Monument Lake, and the ground had been worn away by years of campers. It was too dark here, among the trees, to use the moonlight, so Dan turned on his lamp. The campsite was not occupied, but he could see a few odds and ends left around by previous groups. A rusty grill lay near the fire ring, and a few scraps of foil flickered in the light of his headlamp.

There was a sad, abandoned look to the camp, and Dan and Kristen spent little time there. They walked through an opening in the trees on the far side and were quickly at the edge of the stream where it emptied into the lake.

The other group was out of sight, probably working through the alders that covered the east side of the stream.

Kristen began to walk up the side of the stream, following its course towards Upper Monument Lake. As Dan turned to follow, he noticed something moving in the alders on the far side of the river. There, among the roots of the huge bushes, something small and furry was struggling.

Dan called Kristen over to his side and asked her to point her more powerful light towards the alders. In a flash the animal was gone, leaping out of sight among the bushes. But where it had been, Dan could see something lying on the ground. He stared for a moment before he recognized it. It was Rafael's fishing creel.

He looked for a way to cross the stream, and stepped on one rock, then another. But at that point he ran out of options. From here to the far bank was too far to leap, and he really didn't want to get wet. Not again. Then he thought of his muddy boots and turned to Kristen.

"I guess I'm going to wash off my boots," he said. And he calmly waded into the slippery stones of the creek.

The current always surprised Dan—that and the icy temperature. The water seemed so clear that it would be weightless, but the pressure on his legs forced him to concentrate on every step. Kristen held her flashlight to help him see the way, but it still took a few moments for him to work his way across.

When he got to the far bank, he kicked his boots against a rock to knock some of the water off, then leaned into the alders to try and recover the creel. With a branch pressed into his face, he stretched his arm forward and reached to catch one side of the bag, then tried to drag it towards him. It was caught on a broken root, and it took him a few minutes and more effort that he expected to pull it free.

In the light of his headlamp, he inspected the bag. It certainly looked like Rafael's creel. And inside he could see there were still the gleaming bodies of the trout. This time he counted them. Eight. They had all lost their color now, and none showed the tinge of pink that he had seen on some of them earlier in the day. They were stiff, frozen in death.

He turned and looked at Kristen, showing her the bag.

"Is that Rafael's?" she asked.

He nodded. He could hear, behind him, the crashing of bushes as the other group struggled through the alders to get to the creek. He turned to face them, using his light as a signal to show them where he was.

Cal was the first to push through the branches. His light first flashed on Dan's face, then down to the bag in Dan's hand.

"So where's the fisherman?" he asked Dan.

Dan shook his head. "We didn't see anything on our side of the lake," he said.

A voice called out from behind Cal. "Did you find him?" The rest of the family didn't want to clamber through the alders unless they had to do so.

Cal looked at Dan. "We didn't see anything either. I've got a call in to have someone check the trailhead, to see if his car is still there, but I haven't heard anything yet." He turned away from the stream and said, "I'll meet you back at camp. Maybe we'll see something from this direction that we missed on the way over here."

Then, to the others, he yelled, "No! We found his creel, but he isn't here!"

Dan turned and looked at Kristen. She was sitting on a rock near the stream, waiting. He thought about trying to find a place to cross the stream without getting his feet wet one more time. He could see what looked like a possibility just upstream from where he was, but it would require struggling through the alders to get into position to tell.

With a sigh, he stepped straight into the water and waded back towards Kristen.

During the walk back to camp, Kristen insisted on using her flashlight, to Dan's annoyance. It was just bright enough to affect his eyes' adaptation to the dark, and after only a few minutes, he decided that he might as well turn on his headlamp as well.

He walked along the top of the log through the muddy section of the trail, and soon they were back above the lake on the rocky section where they had stopped before. Now they could see the other group on the far side of the lake. Dan counted three flashlights and wondered how many of the family were in the group.

It was quiet here above the lake, and Dan stopped for a moment to revel in the view once more. He could hear his breathing, slightly accelerated from the climb up onto the rocks. But he could hear something else. He turned to look at Kristen, but she was shining her light towards their campsite.

They could not see the campsite itself because there were trees in the way, but between those trees they could see flickers of light. Dan realized that what he had heard were people yelling.

With a quick word to Kristen, he adjusted the light on his head and started down the trail to camp, moving as quickly as he could through the darkness and uneven terrain. He knew she would follow, but he didn't feel that he could wait for her. She would come along at her own pace.

His eyes were focused on the small white circle of light in front of him. As he ran, that circled bounced wildly from place to place, and

Dan finally ripped the light off his head so that he could hold it in his hand as he ran.

He was trying to move as quickly as he could, but he knew how easy it would be to trip and fall in the bumpy path. The result was an odd, high-stepping jog that tried to give each foot a chance to find its spot on the ground, then adjust as he moved forward. He remembered a line from his days as a cyclist, "Keep your head on top and the rubber side down," and tried to keep his feet under him.

Once near the camp he began to slow down, trying to see what he might find there. The fire was glowing, bigger than he remembered when they left. He could see two people, maybe Gloria and Veronica, standing with their backs to him nearby. They heard him arrive and spun around to face him.

"What's going on?" he asked.

They looked at each other. Veronica spoke first: "We got attacked by a bear."

Dan quickly looked around the campsite for the bear.

"He's gone now," said Gloria, angrily. "He just came to rip our tent apart."

Dan walked over and inspected the tent. It was ripped open on one side, and the contents had been dragged out onto the ground. One of the sleeping bags was also ripped, and bits of down were floating in the air.

"Were you inside when this happened?" he asked.

"We were down by the lake," Gloria answered. "We thought we might as well look for Rafael, and you guys had all gone farther away. When we came back, we saw the bear tearing into the tent. He was huge!"

Dan folded his arms across his chest and took a deep breath. He knew what had happened, and it made him angry.

"Did you see any sign of Rafael?" he asked.

Both women shook their heads. "Did you?" asked Veronica.

"We found his fishing creel, but that's all," Dan replied.

He looked at Gloria. "What kind of food did you have in the tent?"

In the firelight he could see her look away, then back towards him. "It was just a little cheese and crackers," she said. "I was just having a little snack when Veronica suggested that we check this part of the lake."

Dan nodded. "And you left it in your tent?" he asked.

Gloria nodded.

"That's really a problem, you know," he said. "Now the bear knows there is food here, and your tent and sleeping bag are going to smell like food to the bear all night long. So it's really a problem."

"I'm sorry." Gloria looked appropriately chagrined. "I really didn't think this would happen. What do I do now?

"That's your problem," Dan said with some satisfaction. "It's your tent, and your sleeping bag. And it's your problem. I am going to suggest that you put both of them into a food locker, or hang them from a tree so that the bear doesn't spend all night trying to eat them."

Gloria absorbed this information. "If I do that, where am I supposed to sleep?" she asked him.

"That," said Dan with additional emphasis, "is exactly what I mean when I said that this is your problem."

And he turned and walked towards his tent.

# chapter 15

Dan reached into his pack and pulled out the small sheet of foam he used for a seat cushion. At times like this, he needed all the cushioning he could get. He eased his body down onto the pad, perched on a low rock in front of his tent. The rock he was sitting on was too low, and his knees were too close to his chin for comfort. Before he did anything else, he checked his watch, saw that it was now after 11 p.m., and gave a sigh.

His feet were soaked. The laces on his boots were cold and muddy, and it hurt his fingers to untie the knots, which seemed as if they had tightened up during the nighttime adventure. Each boot took his full concentration, and eventually he got both laces loose. He pulled the two sides far apart, knowing that his wet socks would want to stick inside his shoes.

With a grunt he pulled off his right boot, his foot coming out with a sucking sound. His socks were sopping wet, and his hands were now both wet and muddy. He peeled the wet sock off his foot, and tried to wring it out, holding it away from his body. He squeezed plenty of water out of the sock, but he realized it was probably shot for this trip. After pulling the second boot and sock off, he reached into his pack for a towel and dried his feet as best he could.

In the cool air, his feet were now cold, and he rummaged in his pack for a new pair of warm, dry socks. Slipping them on made such a difference, and he added a fleece jacket. There was no sense in feeling cold. He pulled his camp sandals on over the socks, and slipped out behind the rocks to relieve himself.

As he walked back toward his tent, Dan's mind rolled back over the events of the day. What had started as a slow and pleasant hike back into reality had gone from bad to worse. He couldn't help thinking that if he could get a good night's sleep he would be able to pull things together better in morning. There was too much information, too many complications to ponder. He couldn't seem to put any of the pieces together.

He got back to the tent in time to see Cal and the two Himmel brothers arrive in camp. He watched and listened as Veronica and Gloria told them about the bear's visit, and asked for help. He saw Cal lift his arms and hold out his hands, slowly backing away from the group. Cal was not going to get involved in that problem, either. He turned and walked towards Dan and his bed for the night.

Dan saw Gabriela stick her head out of her tent and start yelling something. After some discussion it looked like she was going to let Veronica sleep with her in her tent. And Peter was rigging some kind of rope to hang Gloria's tent and bag in a tree.

"Quite a family," Cal said to Dan as he arrived at the tent. "Man, and I thought mine was bad."

"My feet are just about done," Dan replied. "What a mess."

Cal stood over Dan, looking down at the ranger. "Are you about ready to get into that sleeping bag?"

"Oh yeah," Dan said. "I'm just watching the show here. So where is Gloria going to sleep?"

"I don't know, and I don't care," said Cal. "But if you're getting in your bag, I could use that rock you're sitting on. I'd love to get these shoes off."

Dan eased his body off the rock, sliding under the edge of the tent. He lay back on his sleeping bag, putting his hands behind his head and letting his back slowly flatten against the ground. "Man, does this feel good!" he said.

"I heard from dispatch," Cal said. "Rafael's car is still at the trailhead. If he ran out of here, he didn't take his car."

"Or his fish," Dan added. "Not that he would worry about that. But he probably had a phone. He could have called someone. If he knew we'd be looking for the car, he'd want to leave that behind."

"I don't know who he'd call," Cal said. "The guy lives in Hungary, for chrissake. Who is he going to know up here?"

Dan thought about this for a minute, and then two men suddenly looked at each other and said, in unison, "His sister."

"Shit," Cal said. He pulled out his radio and called in, asking them to run out to Sophie Himmel's house and make sure her car was there. "And if the car's there, they should ask if they can look in her house for Rafael," he added.

The radio rattled back an affirmative response. "I hate to ask the guys to do that," Cal said, "but what the hell, I'm still working. They can do the same. It would really piss me off if that guy was able to sneak out of here just because we weren't paying attention."

By the campfire, the three remaining members of the Himmel family were still arguing. Dan could hear Gloria saying that she was not going to ask Kristen. And Peter was adamant that he did not have room in his tent. The conversation went on for some time.

Cal looked up and asked Dan, "Do you think she's going to end up sleeping by the fire tonight?"

"It's hard to say what they're going to do," Dan answered, "but I have decided one thing that I am going to do."

"What's that?" asked Cal.

"Tomorrow morning, I am going to hand them a couple of citations," announced Dan. "I am going to cite them for the food in their tent, and not keeping it in a bear container. And if we ever find that SOB Rafael, he is going to get a citation for keeping more than his limit of fish."

"Makes sense to me," Cal agreed.

They watched the conversation at the campfire continue.

Both of the others were now staring at Luke. He turned away from the fire, muttering something the men could not hear. But they heard Gloria's response: a firm and not very friendly, "Thank you, Luke."

And then she followed him to his tent.

Cal's boots were now off, and he was ready to get into the tent with Dan. Dan moved over so that he was on his own sleeping bag, and Cal climbed in next to him, trying to organize his blankets as he did so.

"Are you going to be okay sleeping like that?" Dan asked.

"Oh yeah," Cal answered. "Not that I have a choice. But I've done this before." He looked over towards Dan, whose face was invisible in the darkness. "Besides, if I get cold, I'll just cuddle up against you," he said with a grin.

Dan chuckled. "If you get cold, I've got a down jacket in my pack."

"Nah," Cal replied, "that just wouldn't be the same."

Dan could hear Cal moving, trying to get comfortable in the tent. "This is pretty roomy for a one-man tent," Cal said.

Dan pulled his sleeping bag up around his shoulders and settled in. He was getting sleepy, and it felt lovely. "I never know when I am going to have company," he said. He hoped that Cal would stop talking, so that they could both sleep.

Cal's radio blurped an alarm. As Cal answered it, Dan listened in to the conversation with his eyes closed. Whatever they found out, he wasn't going to let it keep him from sleeping well.

He heard the officer on the other end of the radio say, "That flower car is there; it's in the driveway. So I knocked on the door and talked to Ms. Himmel. I think I woke her up. She did not want me to come inside the house."

Cal asked if he saw any sign of Rafael.

"I couldn't see much," the officer replied, "but she didn't look very nervous or anything. She just looked sleepy. And then she was angry that I woke her up."

"Did she already know about her dad?" Cal asked

"She nodded when I asked her if she knew about the accident," came the answer.

Cal held the radio in his hand while he thought this over.

"Do you think you could get a search warrant?" Dan asked him.

Cal sighed. "I don't know. Based on what? We don't have enough of an idea of what happened to explain it to anyone." He held the radio up to his mouth and said, "Thanks, Donny. I don't think there's anything else to do right now. But do me a favor? Keep your eyes open for that car tomorrow?"

"I'll get the word out," the voice on the radio replied.

"Okay," Cal said. "Over and out."

"Over and out," said the radio.

"Over and out," said Dan Courtwright, rolling over onto his side and closing his eyes. He took a deep breath, let it out slowly, and was asleep before he had time to think about it.

# chapter 16

The coffee in Dan's cup was steaming hot, so hot that it was hard to hold the cup in his hands. He kept shifting it from one hand to the other, trying to keep from getting burned. It was a constant battle; the heat of the coffee seemed to be relentless.

Dan didn't usually drink coffee, but Kristen had offered him a cup, and he didn't want to say no. So he said yes. And now he sat on a log by the campfire, staring into the black liquid and wondering when it would finally be cool enough for him to take a sip.

The morning was cool, almost cold, and Dan had not slept well that night. The bear had come back at least twice. And while the bear hadn't bothered Dan, the yelling and banging from the other campers had interrupted his sleep three times. He could only imagine what kind of night Cal had spent wrapped in a couple of blankets.

The Sheriff had left the tent early in the morning, trying to be as quiet as possible. Dan thought that he might have gone straight down the trail to his squad car, but a few minutes later he saw Cal by the fire ring, trying to start a fire. There was a breeze coming down from the mountains, blowing the smoke down towards the valley.

Within minutes, Cal had managed to start the fire, and a few minutes later, Kristen climbed out of her tent and joined him. Dan thought about sleeping in a bit longer. The sleeping bag was toasty warm, but he saw a chance to speak to the others before the Himmel family was up, and he didn't want to miss that.

It took him only a few moments to pull his clothes on, and soon he was sitting by the fire, nursing the cup of coffee.

"How'd you sleep?" he asked Cal.

"Not good," Cal answered dismissively.

"Were you cold?" Dan asked.

"It was noisy," Cal replied.

Kristen interrupted them to say that she was sorry about the problems with the bear. "I explained to them about keeping all the food in the bear boxes," she said, "but I guess they didn't really believe me."

"Nobody believes it until it happens to them," Dan said, "and then they act like it should surprise us all…"

Cal looked up from the fire at Dan. "Are you going to stay here today, or are you heading out?" he asked.

For some reason, Dan checked his watch before answering. It was a few minutes after seven. "No, I'm going to pack up and leave right after breakfast." He looked at Kristen. "Is that okay with you, Kristen? You said that you had enough food for us, too?"

"Oh, sure," she replied. "I think the group decided last night that we were all going to leave today anyway. They are pretty upset about all of this. And we have food for another couple of days, at least. There's plenty for you."

Dan looked around at the other tents in the area. He could see movement in Peter's tent, and probably Luke's too. They would be up soon. He turned to Cal.

"Do you have any update on Rafael?" he asked.

Cal exhaled slowly, letting the air push between his pursed lips. "I haven't bothered to call them. I doubt that he's going to hang around in Sonora today. My bet is that he is already working on getting on a plane somewhere. And if he does that, we might actually stop him before he can leave."

Kristen handed them each a bowl of instant oatmeal and a spoon. "That will get you started. And I have plenty of oatmeal, if you want another bowl," she said.

Dan had finally got the cup of coffee under control, and he now took the bowl of oatmeal warily between his fingers. To his relief, it wasn't nearly so hot.

Cal asked him if he needed help packing up his tent.

Dan shook his head. "It won't take me but about five minutes to pack that up," he said. "Do you want me to toss your blankets in the pack and carry them down for you? It's a lot easier than holding them in your hands as you hike."

Cal looked surprised. "Sure. That would be great," he said. "Have you got anything that you'd like me to carry for you?"

"No," Dan said. "It all fits in the pack. And I've eaten all the food, so there's plenty of room."

Dan got a sense that Cal wasn't listening. The Sheriff was staring out over the lake, lost in thought. Dan waited.

At last Cal snapped out of his reverie. "Where is his fly rod?" he asked Dan.

Dan thought for a moment. "I don't know. I didn't see it last night. But it was dark."

Cal nodded. "I think I'm going to go look for it after breakfast. I wonder…" He paused. "If a guy makes a run for it, does he take the fly rod, or leave it behind?"

"If it's an expensive rod, I think he takes it," Dan said.

"Maybe," Cal replied. "But it would tell us something about the guy either way, wouldn't it?"

"About who?" Peter Himmel was up and had joined the conversation.

"We were just wondering about your brother," Dan said. "Any idea where he could be?"

Peter shook his head. "No. I mean, he could be anywhere. It's not like him to not come back to camp, but I don't know… have you checked on his car? Is it still at the trailhead?"

Dan started to answer, but Cal interrupted him. "That's a good idea," he said. "We'll look into that. In the meantime, as soon as you get out of here, I think you should file a missing persons report in our offices in Sonora."

Peter nodded. "Yeah. We agreed that Gabby would do that this morning, once we got back to town."

"I think it would be a good idea for you all to go together," Cal said. "That way you can all share what you know, and make sure that we don't miss anything. Even a little thing might be important, and we'd hate to miss something like that."

"Okay." Peter sounded a little doubtful. "I guess we could do that."

"Great," said Cal. "Now, while you guys are having breakfast and packing up, I am going to have one last look around the lake for him." He stopped to look at Dan. "I'll swing back through here if you want, and we can hike out together."

"Sure," Dan said. "But it will only take me a few minutes to pack up."

"That's all right," Cal said. "Take a little time off this morning. Sit around the campfire and take it easy. I'll be back soon."

# chapter 17

Dan wasn't about to take it easy. He had not slept enough the night before, and his head felt fuzzy and sore. He watched Luke make a joke, and Gloria laughed a bit. Peter was eating his breakfast by himself, and he could hear Gabriela in her tent, chattering away on her phone. Veronica still wasn't up yet.

Dan walked back over to his tent and started getting packed. He pulled the tent stakes up from the ground and lifted two of the guy lines so that the tarp folded in on itself as it slowly billowed to earth. He folded it together and rolled it up into a tight package, then slipped it into the stuff bag.

He took his pack and set it on top of a flat granite slab, and then began to stack up the things he had to pack next to it. Usually, at the end of the trip, this was an easy exercise, because the food was gone, and there was always room in the bear can for other things. And that made more room in the pack as a whole.

But this time he had to think about where he was going to put Cal's two blankets. Dan was not someone who just threw things into a pack. He had a system that had served him well for many years, and he enjoyed making sure that his pack was exactly the way he liked it: heavy things towards his back, and low, lighter things on top and further back. It kept his weight balanced and closer to his center of gravity.

He looked at his sleeping bag. It would fit into the bear canister now, but would that be the best place for it? In the end, he put his cook kit there, and put that in his pack first, wedging it tightly into the bottom of the pack. On top of that went his sleeping bag and tarp tent. He stuffed his clothes in down around the tent and bag, making everything snug.

As Dan packed, he took pleasure in the careful logic of the process. Each article had its own place, and he enjoyed fitting everything in as perfectly as possible. He jammed his small inflatable sleeping pad inside the pack and decided that he would roll up Cal's blankets to strap them on the outside of the pack.

But while working through the details of the packing, his mind was also working through the details of the events over the last day. Those events didn't fit so neatly together. If Rafael killed his father, would he really have gone fishing right afterwards? And if that was his plan, why would he have disappeared later?

Dan looked up when he heard Gabriela making an announcement over at the fire ring. She was telling Veronica to get up and get dressed, and calling the rest of the family together. Dan tied one of the blankets underneath his back with the straps there, then perched one on top of his pack and pulled the cover down tight over it. It looked a little odd, but the pack felt solid, and Dan hefted it onto his shoulders to test it. It felt good. He put it down and walked over to the fire ring.

Gloria had slept in her dad's tent, and she was now bent over it, trying to roll it up. She gave a frustrated scream and sat back with her arms across her chest. Dan could see tears in her eyes. Luke came over and rolled up the tent for her, patting her on the leg once he was done.

Peter walked over with his gear ready to go.

"I'm all set here, so I think I am going to go check out the lake," he said.

Dan knew that Cal didn't want any help right now, and so discouraged Peter. "If you guys are going to get packed up and out of here soon, my guess is that a couple of people could use some help," he said to Peter. Dan pointed to Veronica, who was having trouble getting her sleeping bag stuffed into its sack.

Gabriela agreed. "Stay around here," she said to Peter. "I don't want anyone to get lost, and there's lots to do. You could help me with my stuff if you don't know what else to do."

Dan looked to see Gabriela carrying out a complete office from her tent, with computer, phone, and massive battery pack. She looked up at him and snapped, "I run this whole company, and I've got to be in contact at all times."

Then she turned to her family.

"I've got through to the packer," she announced, "and they are sending up some mules to pick up our stuff. We need to get everything packed up so they can collect it. They'll be here about noon, so we need to get everything ready before then.

"That means you, Veronica," she shouted into the nearby tent.

Dan looked at Kristen Gallagher, who was taking all this in.

Gabriela turned to Kristen. We'll get our tents and bags together," she said, "and I expect you to wait for the packer here. That way we can leave when we want to. You'll be paid through the end of today. This trip is over."

Kristen flushed, and her voice was a bit tight in her throat as she responded, "I don't mind staying here to meet the packers; I'll be happy to do that. But you hired me for the week, and I've turned down other jobs to take this one. So it's important that you pay me for the whole week. That's what we agreed on."

Gabriela glared at her. "Fine. But I expect you to make sure that everything is packed up and picked up today. If we are paying you, we expect you to work."

Dan looked at Kristen, who was still embarrassed, while she nodded her agreement. He'd had enough of this family. He turned to Gabriela and asked to see her permit for the trip.

"What do you need that for?" she asked.

Dan waited a moment to respond, mentally taking a deep breath. "I am a ranger in this jurisdiction, and I would like to check your wilderness permit, please."

Gabriela shrugged with a sigh and went into her tent. Within a minute she was back out, with the permit in her hand. She held it out to him and said, "We got it at your office, so I assume that it's all correct. One of your guys filled it out."

Dan read through the permit, checking the dates and destinations, then nodded. "Yep, this is correct. And it says here that you are the leader of the group?"

"I'm the leader of the trip," Gabriela said. "I'm the one who organized it."

Dan nodded. "As the leader, you are responsible for the group as a whole," he said. "That includes food storage and the leaving no trace. Because your group failed to store its food properly, we had a problem with a bear last night. And that bear has now learned that it can find food in tents. I am reporting this, and you will receive a notice that you should either pay the fine or appear in federal court to contest it."

Gabriela was furious, her eyes narrowing into slits as she stared at Dan. Dan stared calmly back at her. She turned on her heel and stomped off. "They're going to fine us for that stupid food in your tent," she yelled at Gloria. "I expect you to pay that fine, since it was your damn fault."

The rest of the family gathered around her, then turned to face Dan.

"You are welcome to contest the fine in court," he repeated, "but we have a zero tolerance policy on this matter. It's too important, both for the people here, and the bears."

Gloria looked at Dan disgustedly and said, "Our father died yesterday, and you still think that this matter is important enough to file a report? We will complain about this to your superiors."

Dan nodded. "I understand. You are entitled to do that. And I am sorry about your father. But I also have to do my job."

He turned and walked back to his pack. He boosted the pack onto his shoulders and tightened the belt. It would be good to get onto the trail, and he thought it would be a good idea to start hiking ahead of the Himmels. He was sure he walked faster than they did, and he didn't want to overtake them on the trail, one by one. If he left now, he could get down to the trailhead and leave them behind.

As he started walking past the fire pit he could see Gabriela talking into her phone. She did not look or sound happy.

He checked to see what Kristen was doing. She was sitting quietly amid her equipment, making eye contact with no one. Dan started to say something, then thought better of it, and walked out of camp towards the trail.

# chapter 18

He slowed down as he approached the bridge, and a careful observer would have noticed that his footsteps were lighter. His eyes scanned the small pool just below the bridge, and he was rewarded with a small plop as a trout took a fly off the surface.

The ring had not disappeared when another fish repeated the trick, slightly further down, at the tail of the pool. He stopped well short of the bridge to watch the two small trout play in the sunlight, taking turns rising to splash upwards into the air. Dan could tell they were small fish by the way they attacked with such abandon. He knew that aggressiveness in daylight wouldn't last. The fish would learn to slow down, to hide in the shadows, or something would eat them—something like that osprey by the lake.

On the bridge his feet made a hollow, booming sound on the planks, but his sudden appearance above pool had already spooked the trout, and they flashed through the water into the darkness under the bridge.

Once across, Dan turned and looked back at the camp. He could still see the buzz of activity, bodies moving back and forth to the campfire, stacking up their things.

And he could easily see Kristen, in her pale rose T-shirt. He never did find the time to ask her to dinner. Actually, he had to admit that he never found the courage. Now it was too late. Maybe he would call her once they were back in town.

The trail turned to the right after crossing the bridge, and soon Dan found himself following the stream through the lodgepole forest. The trail wandered in and out of sunlight just enough to be comfortable in the cool morning.

He could hear the stream to his right pick up speed as it tumbled down the back side of the moraine, a series of small cascades that never quite approached waterfalls but carried the stream down quickly to the valley below.

Once the trail dipped downwards to follow the stream, Dan pulled out his radio and made a call to check in with Sara in the office.

Sara sounded happy to hear from him. "Hi, Dan. Cal Healey was trying to reach you. Did you talk with him? Over."

"Not in the last hour or so, Sara. Can you raise him? Over." As Dan let go of the mike button, he wondered what Cal wanted. Had he found the fly rod?

"Hang on, Dan," Sara responded. "I'm going to try and patch him through."

Dan had expected that this would be a short radio call, but he would have to go back to the lake if Cal needed something. He looked around for a rock or log to sit on. The trail here was through a short grassy section on the hillside, out of the trees in full sun. The only shade was back up the trail about seventy-five yards on the top of the moraine. Dan never liked to go back on a trail, but this time he had to admit it made sense.

He found a fallen log in the flimsy shade of a single pine and sat down without taking off his pack. This was not a rest stop, he reminded himself. Once the call was over he would start back towards the trailhead, walking at least two miles before taking a break. Dan wasn't the fastest hiker, but he liked to keep up a steady pace for an hour at a time before taking a short break. On any given day he covered more ground than many people who walked faster.

The radio crackled to life. "Hey Dan, where are you? Over." Cal's voice was badly distorted, sounding like some strange metal dog barking, but Dan could still make out the words.

He pushed the button and responded, "I'm just past the lake, on my way to the trailhead. What's up? Over."

Cal's next question gave him pause. "Are you alone?" Cal asked. "Is there anyone with you? Over."

Dan looked around for a split second before he realized how silly that was. "Nobody here but us chickens, over," he replied.

Cal's response was all business. "I didn't copy that, Dan. Are you with anyone? Over."

Dan played it straight in reply. "I am all alone. I am not with anyone, over."

Cal's voice again barked with its metallic echo, "Can you remember what Rafael Himmel was wearing yesterday? Over."

Dan thought for a moment, then spoke into the radio. "I remember some dark pants, maybe black jeans? And a red shirt. But he was wearing that khaki fishing vest over the shirt. And a ball cap. What's up? Over."

"Yeah, that's pretty much what I remember, too," came Cal's reply. He paused for a moment, and Dan waited for him to continue. "I'm pretty sure I found his fly rod in the lake, up near where we found his creel last night."

That made sense to Dan. If Rafael had decided to flee, he might have just tossed his rod into the lake rather than lug it on the trail.

Cal's voice came over the radio again. "I may have found Rafael, too. You still there? Over."

"I'm here," Dan responded quickly. "Where's Rafael? Over."

Cal took a moment to answer. "I think he might be floating in the lake. t least, there's something floating in the lake up here that doesn't look like a log. Seems like it could be Rafael. Hang on a couple minutes. I am going to climb up the slope a bit to see if I can get a better view. Was everyone okay in camp this morning? Over."

Dan's mind was spinning through the possibilities that this new information carried. "Everyone in camp seemed pretty normal," he answered. "They were all getting packed up and ready to leave. What can you see? Over."

The radio was silent. If that was Rafael in the lake, what had happened? A heart attack while fishing? Rafael certainly seemed like the kind of guy who could have a heart attack. Dan had once pulled a body out of a river like that. And if Rafael had killed his father, he would have been under a huge amount of stress.

But there was a more sinister possibility: that Rafael had been murdered. And if his father had been murdered, too, then this was getting really complicated. Did Rafael kill his father? Did one of his siblings kill Rafael in revenge? And what had Rafael said about seeing someone in camouflage near the lake? Was there a killer still up at the lake?

Cal's voice came over the radio, startling Dan even though he was expecting it. Cal sounded pensive. "Well, I can't say for sure, but I think we've got a second body up here, Dan. Over."

Dan wanted more details. "What do you see, Cal?" And then, with a sinking heart, he heard himself say, "Do you want me to come up there? Over."

"This thing is thirty-five yards out into the lake, so I can't be sure," Cal said. "And there's a little wind, so the surface is kind of choppy. But if it's not a body, then it's somebody's idea of a joke. Over."

That had not occurred to Dan. He felt a flash on anger as he remembered the inflatable doll from the night before. It seemed longer ago than that. "Do you want me to come up and take a look? I can be there in twenty minutes. Over."

Dan voice came back over the radio. "What I really want is to get a SAR team up here to check this out," he said. "But if it's not a body then I'm going to look like an idiot. Over."

Dan thought about making the obvious joke, then resisted the impulse. He stood up and spoke into the radio as he adjusted his pack. "Cal, I'll be up there in twenty minutes. Over."

Dan looked around for a quick place to stash his pack. There was no need to drag it along for the ride, as it would only slow him down. He slipped it off his shoulders and swung it down behind the pine tree.

Cal's voice called back. "I don't think you can do me much good here, Dan. I'm just going to have to get wet and swim out and see what the hell's going on." Cal paused. He didn't sound happy about going into the lake, and Dan understood why. The water would be very cold this morning. Dan waited for the usual protocol to end the message.

Cal voice came on again. "I think you should go back to the camp, Dan, and keep an eye on things there. If what I am seeing is Rafael, then we could have a real problem up here. If someone is trying to kill this family, they've got a good start on that. I'm worried about the rest of them. Over."

Dan had a sudden shot of fear as he thought of someone stalking the people at the campsite. "I'm on my way there right now, Cal. Over."

Dan started jogging back up the trail, his feet feeling light without the pack.

"Be careful," Cal advised. "We don't know what we've got up here. Try to get everyone together and keep your head on a swivel. Over."

"Will do, Cal," Dan replied. But he was more worried about Cal in the lake. "Take it easy on your swim," he warned Cal. He suspected that he was a better swimmer than Cal and thought about offering to switch roles. "That water is going to be cold. Over."

"Yes, it is," Cal responded. "Healey over and out."

Dan slowly shook his head; a slight smile of admiration flickered across his face. "Courtwright over and out."

It was time to get back to the camp.

# chapter 19

Dan resisted the urge to sprint back up the trail. He knew how long that would last before his chest would be heaving in pain in the high altitude. But the sense of urgency drove him forward up the hill in quick strides. It was a pace he knew he could keep up for the distance back to camp, especially because only the first few hundred yards were uphill. Once over the ridge, the trail would flatten out, and he could speed up a bit.

His conversation with Cal had left him with far more questions than answers. If this was another one of the Himmel family jokes, then Dan was prepared to be furious, and he was sure that Cal would be willing to file all sorts of charges as well. But to Dan it just didn't seem likely. After the scene last night around the campfire, he doubted that anyone in the family, even Luke, would have the guts, or stupidity, to do something like that again.

But the knot in his gut didn't come from the idea of a practical joke. It was Cal's suggestion that someone might be trying to kill the whole family. That thought gave him a deep sense of dread. For all the many parts of his job that he loved, the idea that he was responsible for protecting people up here from a deadly criminal was enough to make him sick. Normally, his job was to protect the wilderness from a few campers. This was altogether different.

Who would want to kill the whole family? Dan knew he was not an expert on international crime, but he had read stories in the newspapers about organized crime in Russia. It was possible that Rafael had somehow offended someone with his dealings in Hungary. Did he try to get additional funding from outside the family for his soccer team? Gambling debts? Dan could envision the scenario, and he didn't like what it meant: a professional killer on the loose around Monument Lake.

But would a Russian Mafia hit man bother to pretend these deaths were accidents? Wouldn't he just line everyone up at the campfire and shoot them in the head? Dan knew what an execution style slaying was, and these didn't fit the bill. Besides, if Rafael was the real target, wouldn't he have been left for last? That's the way they did it in most of the movies Dan had seen. In real life these things were less obvious…

At the same time, the killings seemed so targeted and methodical. First Max Himmel, as if hit by falling stone. Then, quietly, Rafael Himmel on the far side of the lake. Did the killer take pleasure in knowing that he was killing them one by one? Was he waiting to isolate another family member, like a wolf separating a lamb from the herd, to kill again?

Dan didn't feel as if he were in great danger, himself. He thought it likely that the killer was targeting members of the Himmel family. But as he thought through the possibilities, he found himself searching the woods along the trail, looking for any sign of motion or human activity. Just in case. He began walking just a bit more quietly through the woods.

He absent-mindedly patted his hip where he wore his gun. It wasn't there, but he felt the need to check. The last time he had carried it was nearly a year ago November, when he discovered a camp of bear poachers. He had observed them through the trees, as they smoked like chimneys and ate their dinner. When he walked into their camp they were surprised, but not dangerous. Recent immigrants from Asia, they had actually been polite as he arrested them. He had almost felt sorry for them. Then he saw the four bear carcasses, including a cub, and his anger overcame his pity.

But this wasn't the work of a poacher; Dan was sure of that. And while he was well aware of the possibility of pot farms on National Forest land, the elevation was too high and the trail too public for that kind of activity. He looked around again, just to make sure he wasn't missing anything.

Who would want these people dead? Why Rafael and Max? Why not one of the others? Why not all of the others? If those two were dead, why were the other ones still alive? Was it just a lack of time? Lack of opportunity? Lack of motive? And who would have been able to track them into this wilderness? Did they announce their destination to the world, or was it a secret? Dan wondered if somehow, someone in the ranger station had leaked information that would have helped the killer. Or had someone even been paid to do so?

Just as Dan began to realize that his thoughts were getting away from him, he caught a flash of motion up ahead on the trail. He froze, then slowly stepped off the trail, half-crouching behind a fallen tree. He could hear voices approach. They were male, and at least one sounded angry. As he peered up the trail, first Luke and then Peter Himmel hiked into view.

Dan took a deep breath and stepped back out onto the trail. Peter started a bit when he saw Dan, then kept walking briskly towards him.

Dan held out his hand and said, "Hang on guys, I need to talk to you."

Peter stopped, placing a hand impatiently on his belt, and waited for Luke to catch up. When he did, Dan held both of his hands out in front of himself and began to speak.

"We may have a very difficult situation here, guys," he began. "I think we need to go back to camp and make sure that everyone is okay."

Peter and Luke exchanged a glance, and Peter said, "They're okay. They were okay five minutes ago when we left them. And they'll be okay an hour from now when they still won't be ready to leave."

Dan nodded. "Actually, the situation could be a lot more dangerous than you know," he said. "I know that you're anxious to get out of here, but Sheriff Healey and I need you to all stay together as a group. He is going to meet us at the camp in a few minutes, and he'll explain more at that time."

Neither Peter nor Luke made any move to comply with Dan's request. Both stared off into the distance, seemingly lost in thought, deciding what they should do.

Dan pushed one more time. "I'm deadly serious. We don't know exactly what's going on here, but until we can secure this area, we need everyone in one place where we can protect them. And that includes you."

Luke looked at Dan with a bemused expression. "If we're in danger, why is it safer to be together? Wouldn't that increase the risk that we could all die together? Wouldn't we be safe splitting up?"

Dan looked him straight in the eye and replied, "My job right now is to make sure that everyone in your family is safe. And I can't protect people who are spread out all over the forest. I need you to come back to camp with me, and I need you to do that right now."

Luke glanced away from Dan's stare and looked at Peter. Almost imperceptibly his body language changed, leaning slightly back towards camp. Dan took the opportunity to make an exaggerated gesture, offering Luke the chance to lead the way back to camp. Luke hesitated for a moment, then turned and walked back up the trail.

Peter glanced at Luke's back, then at Dan. With a quirky shake of his head he followed his brother back up the trail to the camp.

As they neared the camp Dan strained to count the number of people who were there. There should have been four: Gloria, Gabriela, Veronica, and Kristen Gallagher. He could see at least two, maybe three people, sitting on logs by the fire pit. With each step he tried to see past Luke and Peter to verify the numbers. Gabriela was there, talking on the radio. Veronica and Gloria were sitting next to each other on another log.

Kristen was not there.

Dan's eyes scanned the area, searching for any sign of Kristen.

When Gloria saw Luke and Peter, she greeted them with wide eyes. "Back so soon?" she asked sarcastically.

Gabriela, on the radio, suddenly stopped talking. She watched the men walk into camp and then abruptly ended her radio call.

"What's going on?" she asked.

Luke and Peter nodded at Dan, and Luke said, "Ask Ranger Rick here."

Dan's heart was racing, and his breathing was oddly shallow. He did not see Kristen anywhere. He tried to hide any sign of panic in his voice as he asked, "Do you know where Kristen is?"

Veronica answered, "She got all her stuff packed up a while ago. I think she was going to go down to the lake to wait for the packer."

Dan turned towards the lake, eyes searching for a sign of Kristen. He couldn't see anything from the camp. Should he call out?

His radio burst into life. "Hey Dan, where are you? Over," Cal's voice rasped out of the speaker.

Eyes still searching the lake, Dan responded, "I'm back at the camp. I have everyone here except Kristen. Can you see her from where you are? Over."

The radio was silent for a few moments, and Dan was aware that all of the Himmel family members were staring at him.

"I do not see Kristen from here," Cal responded, "but I can't see much from here. Are you with the rest of the family? Over."

"Affirmative, everyone except Kristen. Over," Dan replied.

"Okay," Cal's voice buzzed, "I was right about what I saw this morning. I am on my way to join you at the camp. Over."

Dan felt the knot in his stomach grow bigger and harder. "I am here with the family," Dan said into the radio. "I don't know where Kristen is. Over."

"Roger that," Cal replied. "I will keep my eyes open for her. You need to stay at the camp with the others. I've called for backup, and they should arrive in the next hour or so. I should be there in about twenty minutes. Do you copy that? Over."

"I copy," said Dan. He lifted his thumb off the radio button as he thought over the situation. He knew he should stay at the camp with the rest of the Himmel family—that he could not leave them in danger to go look for Kristen.

"Healey over and out," Cal's voice shot out of the radio.

Startled, Dan looked back at the family around him and said, "Courtwright, over and out."

Gabriela Himmel stood and walked up to Dan, put her hands on her hips, and said to him, "Just exactly what the fuck is going on?"

# chapter 20

Dan tried to keep his voice calm as he responded to Gabriela. He looked around at the rest of the family and forced himself to speak loudly enough so that everyone could hear him. "That was Sheriff Healey on the radio," he said. "I'm afraid it is some bad news. He believes that he has found Rafael. He was floating in the lake. I am sorry, but he's dead."

There was a stunned silence as the family took this in.

Gabriela was the first to speak. "I want out of here, now," she said. "What do we have to do to make that happen?"

Dan knew that Cal had called for backup, and that it would take some time for that to arrive. "Our first priority is to keep everyone safe," he assured them. "We have requested some additional officers who should arrive in the next couple of hours. Right now we don't have a clear idea of how Rafael died, but we are erring on the side of caution, and proceeding as if there is a threat to the safety of the rest of the family."

Gabriela was not appeased. "I want to get out of here," she repeated, "and if you can't get us a helicopter out of here, I can."

Dan took a deep breath before he answered her. "I appreciate your concern, and I share it. My top priority right now is making sure that everyone here is safe and stays safe. That's why we are going to wait for the additional officers to arrive."

He looked around at the family again. "Can you think of anyone who might want to kill both your father and your brother?"

Luke turned his head away, staring at the dirt, while Peter looked Dan straight in the eye. It was Gloria who sniffed quietly and said, "Dad always talked about making enemies in business. He was the one who liked coming up here because he said he didn't have to worry about some hotel clerk or bellhop who held a grudge."

"We're a highly visible, very wealthy family," Gabriela interrupted. "Of course people are going to notice us, and there are plenty of crazy people in this world. We have closed companies and laid off employees. We have been successful where others have failed. So sure, there are people who don't like us."

"What about Kristen?" Luke asked. "Does anyone know where she is? Are we sure that she can be trusted?"

Dan was grateful for the opportunity to focus on Kristen. "I think it is difficult to consider her a suspect at this point, but I am concerned about her," he said. "Does anyone know where she might have gone?"

Veronica surprised them all by speaking up loudly. "Kristen wouldn't hurt anybody," she said. "And she's been in camp the whole time on this trip."

"Besides," said Peter, "if she wanted to kill us, she could just poison us all with mushrooms, right, Gloria?"

"Unless she just wanted to poison Luke," Gloria responded with a grimace for her brother. "But that wouldn't make her different from about fifty other women..."

"Hey," Dan called the conversation back to order. "When did Kristen leave camp? And where did she go? Did anyone see her?"

"I saw her leave about fifteen minutes ago," Gloria said. "So did Luke," she added pointedly. "He tried to follow her and she asked him to go back to camp. And she went over there." Gloria pointed to the trail that led around the lake on the west side.

Dan thought this over. He was very worried about Kristen, but he didn't want to leave the rest of the family. And he didn't want to ask them to join him on the search—if there was a killer in the area, that was way too risky.

Gabriela was now heard talking on the radio. What had begun as a quiet conversation now became heated, as she learned that getting a helicopter to fly in to help them was going to be more difficult than she imagined.

Gloria started calling out to Kristen, shouting her name towards the lake. Dan appreciated the effort, but he knew how difficult it would be for Kristen to hear them or realize that they were calling her name. Sound does funny things in the mountains.

He spoke up again to the whole group. "Look, we don't have the information we need to really understand the situation here," he said. "Rafael had mentioned someone in camouflage clothing who was near the spot and time where your father died. And now Rafael is dead. If there is someone who is trying to kill you, then it is absolutely critical that we stay together, that we stay very alert, and that we work together to protect each other."

Luke snorted in derision. "Doesn't that make us just one big target, and a lot easier to hit?"

Gabriela put down her radio and responded. "No, he's right. Dad and Rafael were alone, far from the group. We need to stay together."

Dan nodded, and saw his opportunity. "Right," he said. "I need you all to stay together, right here, and keep your eyes open. I want at least three people on watch at all times. Gabriela, can you organize that?"

Gabriela nodded, and before she could speak, Dan continued. "Do not let anyone get close. Stay here, stay together, and wait for me or Sheriff Healey."

"Where are you going?" asked Veronica. "Are you just leaving us here?" She could not keep the indignation from creeping into her voice.

"Cal Healey should be here in a few minutes," Dan replied. "I am going to look for Kristen. And I hope I'll be back soon, too."

He stopped to look at the family. Their faces showed a range of emotions, from fear in Veronica to anger in Gabriela. He thought about staying longer, or saying something to reassure them.

Then he thought about Kristen, and he turned quickly and strode off towards that trail around the lake.

Over his shoulder he could hear Gabriela taking charge, speaking up over the mumbled comments of the others. And as he reached the start of the trail, the last thing he heard was Gloria state with great purpose, "I need something to eat..."

# chapter 21

Dan turned his back on the Himmel family and walked quickly towards the trail around the lake. He could hear them start to protest behind him, but he wasn't going to listen or allow them to delay his search. He knew that Cal would arrive at the camp fairly soon, and he couldn't wait any longer to look for Kristen.

But where to start? He realized that he was headed towards the rocky point overlooking the lake, where he and Kristen had their conversation the night before. Had she felt the same connection that he had felt during that talk? For some reason, Dan felt sure that he would find her there.

Or was he just kidding himself? If she had decided to go off somewhere to be alone, she would certainly have chosen a spot more isolated than that. And she could be anywhere.

As Dan got to the lake he started calling out her name—first once, then a second time, even louder. He waited a few minutes, motionless, to hear any response.

He heard nothing but wind whispering lightly through the junipers on the slope above the lake.

His breath becoming faster, Dan began to jog along the trail by the lake, winding around through the rocks and trees, until he came again to the small meadow before the rocks. He yelled again, twice.

No answer.

Dan realized that he had never come right out and told Kristen that he found her so attractive, so interesting. That felt stupid now, and he began to run a little faster, as if by running faster he could somehow make that point to her: that he didn't want to lose her.

He had never kissed her. Had never told her he cared about her. But he was frantic not to lose her now.

The trail through the last part of the meadow was damp and muddy, and Dan stopped in front of the line of logs that hikers had placed there. He would not be able to run along these so quickly. He stared ahead at the rocks and called out again, "Kristen!"

When he heard no answer, he began to walk along the first log. And then he heard something. A voice?

He stopped, balancing along the log, and called again. "Kristen?"

Her voice came from somewhere ahead of him in the rocks. "Looking for me?"

Dan couldn't see her, and stopped to search among the rocks for her face.

"Is the pack train here?" Kristen called out to him.

Dan took a huge gasp of breath and leaned forward, placing his hands on his knees to rest. He tilted his head up and asked, "Where are you?"

"Up in the rocks above you..." she called out. As he looked up, he saw just her head above the rocks, a good fifty yards away.

"You need to come back to the camp right away!" he called out. "Cal Healey found Rafael. He's dead, in the lake on the other side. We're afraid that there might be a serial killer out here!"

Dan paused for a moment. "You really have to come back to the camp with me, Kristen. Quickly!"

For some reason, Kristen did not respond immediately. When she did, she called out, "Okay, but don't come up here." And then, after another short delay, "I'll be down in a minute."

Alarm bells began to sound in Dan's head. He didn't like that answer, and he began first to trot, then to sprint up the rocks towards Kristen. If someone was up there with her, he had to move fast to make sure she was safe. As he ran, he called out, "Are you okay?"

Again a pause, and Kristen's answer sounded a bit muffled. "Yeah…"

Was she already struggling with someone? Dan could feel his breath begin to pant as he ran and hopped up into the rocks. Thoughts raced madly through Dan's brain. If the killer were nearby, and heard Dan's comments, would he now kill Kristen? Did Dan's words cost Kristen her life?

Leaping from granite ridge to boulder, Dan sprang up the rocks and suddenly towered over Kristen. She was in a sunny hollow in the rocks, quickly pulling her shirt over her head. A baby blue T-shirt. And her bra was white.

As Kristen's head poked through her shirt, she stared up at Dan and scowled. "Do you mind?"

Dan spun around and stared off into the lake, trying hard to act like he was interested in the water. "I'm sorry," he choked out. The Monument was directly across the lake from him, a witness to his awkwardness. His cheeks flushed bright pink from embarrassment. Dan felt such a fool. Now Kristen must think he was just like Luke.

"Okay, I am decent," she said quietly to him.

"We really need to get back to camp," Dan began. "The rest of the family is there, and Cal should be there by now, too. And backup is on the way; Cal called for some help. That should be getting here soon." He could feel himself talking too much, still staring off into the lake.

But he couldn't seem to stop talking. "What were you doing out here? Why were you so far so far from camp?" As he asked these questions, he slowly turned, making sure that Kristen really was fully clothed.

"I was sunbathing," she said, "and I didn't want to be disturbed..."

Dan fell into silence. He could feel his ears burning. "I'm sorry," he said. "I just wanted to make sure you were safe..."

Kristen stared hard at Dan, and he looked away again. "Do you think there really might be someone trying to kill us all?" she asked.

Dan took a deep breath before answering. "We don't really know. But we've got two very suspicious deaths on our hands, and so far we don't have any answers. One of the possibilities is that there is someone up here who is killing people. And we don't know who, or why."

Kristen thought this over. "And you came out here to find me?"

Dan nodded. "Yeah."

Kristen held out her hand to him, so that he could help her up onto the rocks. "Thanks, that was sweet of you," she said.

"Okay..." Dan felt a sudden surge of warmth in his chest and a slight difficulty in talking. "We'd better get back to camp now," he said.

As they began to work their way down the rocks, Dan found himself wanting to help Kristen at every point. Twice he held out his hand to offer her support. The first time, she took his hand and steadied herself on a ledge. The second time, she ignored it.

Dan wasn't sure what that meant.

As they got to the meadow, Dan's radio came to life.

"Dan, this is Cal. I'm back at the camp. Where are you? Over."

"Just a couple of minutes away, Cal," replied Dan. "I have found Kristen, and she is okay. We are on our way back to camp. Is everyone there? Over."

"All present and accounted for," Cal answered back. "I am going to get things organized here. I'm happy to hear that you found Kristen. Over."

"Me too," said Dan. "Over and out."

Quietly, Dan heard Kristen's voice behind him on the trail. "Me too," she said.

She was breathing hard, but nodded, then stuck her tongue out like a dog panting, and smiled at him.

Dan turned and started to walk through the woods. The trail went uphill a little bit here, and he took it very slowly. He found it easier to think like a musician, with each step taking two beats, instead of one. He realized that he was doing what he always did on the trail; he was letting his mind wander while his body worked. It was a beautiful kind of therapy, but it was the wrong thing to do right now.

He brought his mind back to the woods around him.

At the top of the little ridge there was a wide spot in the trail, and he paused and looked back again. Gloria was now fifteen or twenty feet behind him, and laboring hard. Veronica, on Gloria's heels, was clearly frustrated. Dan waited for the whole group to catch up, then asked if everyone was doing okay. It wasn't really a question, and they knew it. It was just a short stalling tactic to allow Gloria a few more seconds of rest on top of the ridge.

He counted to ten, then began to lead the group down through the forest to the meadow below. He found himself thinking that this was the first time in the last two days that he had heard such silence from this family. For once they were not arguing...

A scream from behind him snapped him out of his thoughts.

"There!" Veronica screamed again. "What's that there?!"

Dan froze in place, his arms out behind him, waving to the group to get down. From behind him he heard Cal Healey yelling, "Get down! Everyone get down!"

As Dan bent down in a crouch, he turned and looked at Veronica. She was still pointing down the trail ahead. Dan followed her gaze and found himself looking down at his own backpack.

# chapter 23

Dan slowly stood up, making eye contact with Cal Healey. "It's okay," Dan said quietly. "That's my pack. I just left it here when you called so that I could get back to camp quicker."

Cal's eyes continued to search the forest, while the others in the group slowly stood back up again and looked around. "Everybody okay?" Cal called out from behind.

The Himmel siblings all looked at each other and mumbled their assent. Before anyone could criticize Veronica, Cal called out to her directly. "Veronica, that was just what you are supposed to do. Good job. I know it was a false alarm, but you did exactly the right thing there."

Veronica looked somewhat embarrassed, whether from the false alarm or the compliment, Dan couldn't really tell. He turned to her and said with a smile, "It was good practice, anyway."

Veronica nodded, still not making eye contact with him.

"Let's hope that's all we see on this trail," he added. He walked forward to his pack and picked it up. There was no reason to leave it here, and it wouldn't slow him down on the trail, at least not enough to matter. Not with Gloria setting the pace.

Dan turned to the rest of the group and asked if they were ready to move on.

Gloria raised her hand. "I know this isn't really the right time or place," she said apologetically, "but I really, really have to pee."

Dan shot a look at Cal, who rolled his eyes. The two of them began to search the area around the trail, trying to determine if it would be safe enough to send Gloria into the woods. Dan could see that Cal was frustrated by the request. There was a long silence as the two of them thought it over.

It was Cal who spoke first, after blowing his cheeks out with a big sigh. "Okay, I'm going to go off to the left here and do a little recon. Wait here until I get back."

The three Himmel daughters found a log just off the trail, and sat down to wait—Veronica having to shift over a bit to make room for Gabriela. Peter and Luke remained standing, hands on hips, and staring down the trail towards the meadow below. Kristen pulled a small water bottle from her hip belt and took a quick drink.

Dan thought for a minute, then slid his pack back off his shoulders and let it slip to the ground. He leaned it against a tree near the trail. There was no need to carry it until they were underway again. He could hear branches crack where Cal was walking up through the forest on the left-hand side of the trail.

After a few minutes, Cal called out to the group. "Hey, guys, I think it's okay if you want to come up to this side a bit. I'm up above you, and I'm going to keep watch over here. But I think you can find a little privacy in some of those manzanitas, if you want."

Gloria turned around to see where Cal was standing. It was obvious to Dan that she couldn't quite pick him out, and that she was feeling awkward about the situation. Slowly she stood up and began to walk into the forest. "Where are you?" she called out to Cal.

"Don't worry," Cal answered her. "If you can't see me, I can't see you. But I am keeping watch up here."

Gloria slowly walked up into the manzanita bushes, turning to check on her position, trying to find a spot that was hidden from the trail and also hidden from Cal. Dan didn't envy her task.

Peter suddenly turned to Dan and said, "I'm going to take a leak, but I'll just go on the other side of these trees right here." The three trees he pointed to were only ten or fifteen feet from the trail.

Dan nodded, and advised him, "Okay, but stay close." Kristen walked slowly down the trail towards Dan, giving Peter a little more privacy.

Cal called out from above, "Everybody okay?"

Gloria suddenly appeared in the manzanita bushes and began walking back to the trail. As she did so, Dan could hear Cal moving in brush and forest above them. Behind the trees, Peter gave a sneeze.

Dan turned his glance to Kristen. She met his gaze and was about to say something when there was a bang, then a shout from Peter.

"Ow! Hey! What the fuck?" Peter came stumbling back out onto the trail. Luke raced up to meet him. Peter's hands were holding the left side of his head. Luke was trying to reach him to see what had happened.

As Dan and Kristen walked towards Peter, he could hear Cal crashing down the slope above them, and over the crashing bushes he heard Cal calling out, "What happened? What's going on?"

Peter stopped and pulled his hands away from his ear. Dan could see blood on Peter's face and neck, dripping down onto the shoulder and neck of his shirt.

"Oh my God, he's bleeding!" Gabriela shouted.

"Get down, get down!" Cal was yelling from above them. "Everybody get down!"

The women on the log scrambled off their seats and slowly slid down on the ground, eyes wide with fear. Peter slowly dropped into a crouch, with Luke beside him. Luke put an arm around Peter and then looked back over his shoulder into the forest.

Dan bent low at the waist and crept quickly towards the two men. He could see now that it was Peter's ear that was bleeding profusely. He patted his shirt pockets, searching for a tissue or his bandanna. But he knew the bandanna was in his pack. As he turned to go back for it, Kristen handed him a soft yellow bandanna from her pants pocket.

"Thanks," he said quietly, then turned to Peter.

The ear had a deep nick in the edge. As Dan applied the bandanna to the ear, he asked Peter, "What happened?"

Cal clumped down onto the trail from above, and in a few big strides was standing next to them, eyes focused on the forest above them, his pistol in his hand.

Peter shook his head. "I don't know. I was just on the other side of this tree. I was done peeing, and then I sneezed. And there was this bang, and it seemed like the tree behind me kind of exploded. And my ear hurt like hell."

Dan pulled the bandanna away from the ear to look at it again. "Something took a chunk out of your ear," he said.

Cal reached out to put a hand on Dan's shoulder, keeping the bandanna away long enough for Cal to look at the ear as well.

"Something dinged you good," he said. And as he said it, his body slid lower and lower towards the ground, and he eased himself behind one of the big trees. His eyes were now back scanning the forest above them. As he studied the trail above, Cal started speaking to Dan in a quiet voice.

"Dan, I need you to get these people down the trail a bit, maybe behind those logs off to the left. Keep your head down, and get moving."

There was no mistaking the tension in Cal's voice.

Dan turned to Kristen, and then jutted his chin towards the three women who were now half-lying on the ground behind them. "Can you get them around the corner of the trail into those trees?"

Kristen, already down on her knees, agreed and quickly crawled down the trail towards Gloria and her sisters.

Dan looked at Luke. "You go first. Peter and I will follow you."

Luke nodded and immediately crawled off after Kristen.

Cal was still watching the forest above them, but spoke quietly to Peter and Dan. "We don't know how many of them are out there," he said. "So I am going to try and stay here. I hope there is only one, so I can manage that. But I need you guys to really pay attention. If you see or hear anything down below, give a shout… and I mean a shout."

Peter was now holding the bandanna on his ear, and he pulled it away, only to see it covered in blood. He quickly replaced it and turned to Dan. "What the hell happened there?" he asked.

Cal never took his eyes from the forest, but answered Peter in a quiet voice. "Looks like you got shot, Peter. The good news is that they basically missed."

Peter stared at Dan, bewildered. "But I didn't hear anything. How could I get shot without hearing anything?"

"Yeah," said Cal, still alert to the forest above. "Exactly. Get moving, guys. This is no joke."

Dan encouraged Peter to move down the trail. Peter, with one hand holding the bandanna on his ear, scurried down the path, bent well over and not stopping to look back.

Looking out at the forest with Cal, Dan asked him, "What's your plan here?"

Cal snorted quietly. "I don't have a fucking plan. My plan is to try and keep those people alive, at least until the backup arrives."

Dan stared out at the forest next to Cal. "This sucks," he said. He hoped to keep the fear out of his voice but wasn't sure that he had.

"Sure does," Cal replied, and Dan could hear the fear there, too.

"Go on, get down there with those folks and make sure they don't do anything stupid," Cal said to Dan.

"Okay," Dan agreed. "Be careful here, huh?"

"Oh yeah," said Cal. "That's definitely part of the plan."

# chapter 24

Dan crept down the trail, leaving Cal behind. He was bent low at the waist, trying to give as small a target as possible as he moved. After nearly a week in the backcountry, his back and knees were not happy with the developments, and by the time he reached the rest of the group his breath was coming in gasps. He collapsed down next to Luke behind the first log and caught his breath.

Gabriela called over to him. "What's going on?" she demanded. "Who is doing this?"

Dan rolled over so that he could see her. For once she looked more scared than commanding. Dan looked around at the other faces. Gloria was lying on the ground, as if she were trying to burrow right under the log. Veronica was wedged in next to her, looking a bit resentful that Gloria had better protection.

Kristen and Gabriela had each found a tree, and were sitting up, legs straight out in front of them and with their backs to the trees, while they looked at Dan and waited for an answer.

Peter had moved up the hill above them, just enough to get behind a couple of smaller chunks of granite. He was still holding his ear with his right hand. And Luke was crouched next to Dan; he was watching the trail up above, and glanced down at Dan.

Dan shook his head. "We don't know. We don't know who is out there, or how many might be out there." He thought about it for a moment, then added, "You might have a better idea of who's out there than we do. All we know is somebody took a shot at Peter. We don't know who or why."

He looked at Peter, who pulled his hand away from his ear to check the bandanna. It was now soaked with blood. Dan heard Peter swear quietly and refold the bandanna so that he could place a relatively clean part of the cloth against his ear.

Gabriela spoke up again. "So what are we supposed to do now?" She was speaking in a kind of stage whisper, loud enough to reach everyone in the group, but perhaps not loud enough to be heard by anyone out in the forest.

"We stay safe," Dan replied. "We stay behind these logs and trees, and we keep our eyes open. Cal is up above, and he's going to make sure that nobody gets past him."

"Shouldn't we try to get out of here?" Gabriela asked.

"If you look downhill, you can see that meadow," Dan replied. "No trees, no logs, no protection. So we're better off here." He knew this to be true, but it wasn't much consolation. "We've got backup on the way, and we're just going to wait for it to arrive."

Dan heard Peter give an enormous sigh, and then slouch down behind the rocks. It looked as if he were lying down now in the manzanita; only his boots were visible to the left of the rocks.

The minutes passed. Dan raised his head slowly, and joined Luke in watching the trail above. He could just see the bottom of Cal's right leg and foot further up the trail as the Sheriff kept watch. The sun was warming now, and Dan could feel the heat rising from the meadow below them. It was going to be a hot day.

A squirrel chattered away in a tree off to the left. Dan wondered if it was because someone was walking over there… or if the squirrel was chattering at them. He strained to look, but there were too many trees in the way, and he could see nothing.

A fly buzzed near Luke's head, and Luke waved his hand to brush it away. The fly returned.

Gloria, behind him, suddenly whispered, "Shit, there are ants everywhere here!" Dan turned to see her wriggling out from under the log, brushing off her hands and arms.

Peter's voice came down from the bushes. "They won't bite," he reassured her. "They're not fire ants or anything. They're harmless."

"But I don't like them!" Gloria's voice was edging towards panic. She and Veronica were now both swatting and brushing at the ants.

"Shhh!" Kristen hushed them. "Be still. I hear something."

The group sat still and silent, ears straining to hear what Kristen had mentioned. At first Dan only heard the gentle hum of insects in the meadow. Then, somehow beneath that, he heard another noise, something deeper and heavier.

Kristen suddenly turned towards him. "It's the pack train! They're coming into the meadow!"

Dan turned his head down the hill and watched through the trees. He could see the trail in the lower part of the meadow. Sure enough, the first horse of the pack train came into view, steadily walking up the trail towards them.

He quickly spoke to the others. "I've got to go let them know what's going on," he said. He turned up the trail and called out to the Sheriff, "Cal—pack train is in the meadow. I'm going down to meet them."

Cal didn't turn around, but slowly waved his arm behind him where Dan could see it. Then Dan's radio came on. "If we can get those horses up here, it would help us get these people out of here," he heard Cal speaking quietly from the radio.

"Yep, got it," Dan responded.

Dan moved into a crouch behind the log, then set his sights on the trail below and began to sprint down into the meadow to meet the pack train. As he neared the horses, he held his hands up to stop the procession. Dan recognized Luis Aguilera as the packer—a young cowboy from northern Mexico who had quite a reputation as a trick rope specialist. "We've got someone shooting at people up here," he called out to Luis. He could see Luis' eyes open wide at the news.

Dan now stood in front of the pack train, breathing hard. "We've got a bunch of people up there just inside the forest," he explained, "and we need to get them out."

Luis seemed to be frozen in place. He listened attentively to Dan but made no move, except to turn around a look at the five horses behind him. Then he looked back at Dan.

Dan spoke again. "We've got to get these horses up into the forest, so they can shield the people as they walk out."

Still no movement from Luis. It occurred to Dan that Luis didn't know what Dan expected of him—and he didn't like the idea of getting off his horse.

"I think you would be safer on foot," Dan said. "A smaller target. Let's walk the horses up into the forest and get the people out. There are four women and three more men," he said.

It may have been Dan's imagination, but Luis responded with a start to the mention of the women. Dan smiled at the thought that chivalry might not be dead after all.

Dan didn't want to lead the horses, because whoever was in front of the pack train would be too obvious a target. He pointed uphill and explained, "We think the shooter is over there, to the left and above, so we have to be really careful getting in there. I'd rather have a horse take a bullet than you or me."

Luis thought about this for a minute, then offered, "I can ride on the side of this horse. He'll let me do that. He's a good horse." Luis waited for this to sink in. "Then you can walk back there, next to the next horse."

Dan watched as Luis suited action to words, and quickly slipped off the saddle and put all of his weight on his right leg, then lowered his body so that he was mainly hidden behind the body of the horse, his weight on the right stirrup. He held the reins loosely in his left hand.

Luis turned his head to look at Dan and smiled. "You ready?"

Dan shook his head in amazement and said, "Yep. I'm ready."

Luis urged the horse forward and Dan started walking along the trail next to the second horse in line.

Dan reached out and grabbed a rope on the pack of the horse. As he did so he noticed the butt of a rifle sticking out of the pack. "Hey, Luis," he said. "I think it would be a good idea to get this rifle out where we can use it."

Luis looked back over his shoulder. "I don't have any ammo," he said. "The horses don't like the noise. I just bring it to make the people feel better."

"Can I pull it out?" Dan asked.

"Yeah, sure," Luis replied.

"Good," said Dan. "It just might help the people feel better."

# chapter 25

As a hiker, Dan had never been a big fan of horses on the trail. A single horse creates as much wear and tear on a trail as a hundred hikers, and that really doesn't count the massive damage they do to meadows and campsites. But today all that seemed beside the point. Dan's hand held the side of the pack while the horse next to him provided fifteen hundred pounds of walking cover on the trail. Dan was happy to walk alongside, stomping through the grass of the meadow, and keeping himself safely out of the line of fire. He could feel the solid weight of the horse through the soles of his boots.

He spoke quietly to Luis as the two moved forward through the meadow into the forest. "Let's walk these horses right past the people up here, until we get up to where Cal Healey, the Sheriff, is. I want to try and get everyone out of here…"

Luis turned around and looked at Dan. He thought about what Dan had said, then nodded. "Okay, I'll ride up to the Sheriff, and then we'll make some plans." But Dan could see that he wasn't excited about the idea.

Dan didn't want Luis to run any unnecessary risks, and warned him, "Take your cues from Cal. Just make sure you keep that horse between you and the shooter up here."

This time Luis replied with a smile. "Don't worry, I'll stay behind this horse the whole way, okay? You just tell me where to ride. I'll take the horses just where you say."

As they reached the edge of the meadow, Dan could see Gabriela Himmel up the trail ahead, waving to him. "What an idiot," he said to Luis. "She's going to get shot waving to us."

"I think she is just happy to see us," Luis replied.

Gabriela continued to wave frantically. "She is really happy to see us," Dan said with a shake of his head. He couldn't imagine what was going through the woman's mind.

Luis turned around to comment to him, but his gaze quickly focused on the meadow behind them. "What's that?" he asked Dan.

Dan turned to see another group of three riders enter the meadow. It took him only an instant to recognize the three as members of the Sheriff's Department. With his right hand he reached down and pulled out his radio.

"Courtwright to Healey, over," he broadcast, then waited for Cal to reply. The wait seemed too long to him, and he was just about to call again when Cal came on with a reply.

"Hey, Dan, see anything? Over."

Dan breathed a sigh of relief. "Your backup arrived. We've got three deputies down below coming into the meadow on horseback. Are you doing okay? Over."

"Okay so far," Cal replied. "But don't let those guys ride up here on their horses. Get them down on foot and into cover. Over."

"Roger that," Dan replied. He looked at Luis. "Let's wait for these guys," he said. "They know what they're doing, and we can use the extra firepower."

Luis didn't say anything, but eased himself out of position on the saddle and gently dropped to the ground next to his horse. Dan could see Luis was relieved at the sight of help on the way. Dan asked him to hold the horses there, while the ranger turned and loped off to meet the three deputies.

It didn't take him long to summarize the situation. "We think there's at least one shooter in the woods, above the group. Cal's behind a couple of big fir trees up there, and he's armed and holding that position. The rest of the group is down below here, just inside the forest."

"First things first," responded the young man on the lead horse. His nametag said his last name was Irwin; Dan hadn't met him before. "Let's get those people down to the trailhead and out of here. And while we do that, let's give Cal some backup," he said. "If we get ourselves up there and in position with Cal, can you get the civilians across this meadow and back down the trail?"

"That was the plan before you got here," Dan replied, "but it's going to seem a lot easier with you guys here."

"Good," replied Deputy Irwin. He slid off the saddle and dropped to the ground. "So, guys, we are just going to walk our horses up to where Sheriff Healey is. When we get there, we'll set up a defensive position, and cover the ranger here while he gets these people out. Is that clear? Any questions?"

The deputy in the back pulled out a shotgun from his saddle and quickly loaded it. The other two moved forward and Dan followed them up to Luis and the pack train. As they walked, Deputy Irwin said, "We passed one of your guys on the way in. He's on foot, but he was making good time. You should meet him as you go back down the trail."

Dan thanked him; it was good to know he'd find extra help along the way.

When the four men reached the pack train, Dan asked Luis, "Can you take these horses up to where the people are now, Luis? These guys are going to go up to Cal's position, and once they get there, it will be easier for us to get the people out."

Luis nodded. "It's nice to see you guys," he said with a shy smile.

"Yeah," said Deputy Irwin, "We get that a lot." And with that he and his two colleagues started walking their horses up out of the meadow and into the woods toward Cal Healey.

Dan waited with Luis down in the meadow. Here the sun beat down until he was sweating. It had been three days now since he had bathed, and his whole body felt filthy. The horses waited patiently, occasionally flickering a muscle to scare the flies away. Luis, now sitting on the ground next to his horse, slowly fanned his face with his hat. At first they could hear the noises of the group of deputies moving into the forest, but then all grew silent. Finally, Dan's radio crackled with the sound of Cal's voice. "Hey, Dan, we're in position up here. I haven't seen anything at all, but let's not take any chances. If you can get these people out of here, that will make our jobs a lot easier. Go ahead and move them out. Over."

"Got it, Cal," Dan replied. "We're going to head up and circle the horses around them. Then we'll walk the horses back out, shielding the people. Over."

Luis climbed back into position, riding on the right side of the lead horse. Dan thought it was possible that Luis was just showing off, but if he had practiced this trick for years, he had certainly found the time and place to use it. Within minutes they were walking up the trail beside the Himmel family and Kristen Gallagher.

"Just stay down, everybody!" Dan insisted. "Stay where you are! When we are ready, we'll let you know and get you out of here."

He looked on as Luis slowly circled the horses and turned them back down the trail. As he did so, he eased his body up over the saddle and then down on the other side of the horse. Dan couldn't help but smile a bit.

When Luis was ready, Dan spoke to the group. "Let's get everyone in place here. You need to be walking right next to a horse, and in line with his front legs. Once we get down into the meadow, we can regroup." He watched as all five Himmels quickly found themselves spots next to horses and stood waiting. Dan realized that he was the odd man out. He turned to Kristen and said, "Why don't you go up and walk next to Luis on the lead horse? I'll go here."

Dan reached down for his radio and called Cal. "Are we good to go?"

"Yep," Cal responded. "We've got you covered. Just get them out of here."

Dan shot a quick look at Luis, and the packer started forward slowly, easing the horses down out of the forest and into the meadow below. Their progress seemed painfully slow, but Dan realized that his adrenaline was now fully engaged, without any real use. With a focused effort, he forced himself to walk slowly at the side of his horse, shuffling along next to the trail through the meadow, and down into the forest below.

# chapter 26

It was more than three miles to the trailhead, and as Dan checked his watch he realized that at this rate it would take them almost two hours to get there. Even with his pack, Dan could cover the same ground in an hour, maybe less. At least they were now back in the forest, where the shade kept the temperatures cooler.

His radio kept him informed on developments up above in the forest. At first it had been silent, but then Dan heard short snippets of communications. He could tell that the sheriffs had now split up, and were beginning to fan out through the forest, looking for the shooter.

He'd never been on that kind of a mission. He knew the training, but real life was so very different. He could only imagine the tension up there as they worked from one tree to the next, each bush or rock holding the potential sniper. How much territory would they have to cover before they found him? And what would they do if they didn't find him?

A commotion on the trail up ahead captured his attention. As the horses dragged to a halt Luis called back to him, "There's a ranger up here looking for you!"

Dan let go of his horse's pack and jogged forward. He should have known it would be Ralph Gephart on the trail in front of him. Slow, phlegmatic, with a penchant for following every rule and a mind closed to any possible creativity, Gephart was Dan's least favorite colleague. And he often bragged about how his gruff nature resolved every conflict in his favor.

"What's your plan here, Courtwright?" Gephart asked him.

"Hi, Ralph." Dan shook his hand. "We're just walking these people out of here. The Sheriff's Department is up above Monument Meadow, and they're dealing with the situation up there." Dan was more than a little worried to see that Ralph was wearing his sidearm.

"Well," Ralph began importantly, "do you need me here, or should I go up and help them?" You could tell by the way he said it that he really, really wanted to get up into the action.

"My orders from them were to get these people to safety," Dan said. He realized that he needed something for Ralph to do, or the older man was quite capable of walking back up to the crime scene. And if that happened, Dan was not sure the result would make Cal very happy. He looked at Ralph Gephart and suggested, "We don't have anyone at the front of this line. Luis is managing the horses, but if you could go ahead of him and clear the area first, that would really help us."

Ralph looked around at the group and nodded. Then he turned to the packer. "Okay, Luis, you just follow me," he said. "Wait for my signal to move forward."

Dan watched as Ralph Gephart walked fifty feet down the trail, then motioned the pack train forward. Slowly the horses edged forward, then slowed again. Gephart's hand was raised to halt them. Another motion forward.

Dan sighed. He looked at his watch. It was going to be more like three hours. He sighed again. Maybe three and a half.

# chapter 27

In fact, things on the trail were not going well. Dan could see that the women in front of him were having real trouble staying next to the horses, and as they got further along the trail, that would only get harder. In the meadow this hadn't been a problem, but now that there were trees and rocks to dodge, it was getting impossible.

When he checked on Peter and Luke behind him, he wasn't really surprised to see that they were now walking behind the horses, rather than next to them. When Dan caught their eye, the two men just shrugged and continued to follow the horses down the trail.

Now the trail began to slowly work its way down the steep face of the moraine below the meadow. He heard a loud squawk from in front of him, then saw Luis quickly turn around and stop the horses.

Amid the commotion, Dan hurried forward and looked over Kristen's shoulder. Veronica had apparently tripped on a tree root and fallen down, ending up underneath the horse next to her.

"This isn't working," Gabriela pointed out to him.

Dan nodded. "The trail is only going to get steeper and narrower here," he agreed. "And there's no way we can walk next to these horses on the switchbacks." He stared off into the forest, trying to come up with a solution.

Kristen helped Veronica back to her feet and dusted off her clothes. "Are you okay?" she asked.

Veronica looked at her gratefully and shuddered. "A little shaken up, but okay," she said. She held her elbow and rubbed it. "I think I got kicked on the elbow."

"You're lucky you didn't get stepped on," Kristen said, continuing to brush dust off Veronica's back and legs.

Ralph came running back to the group, pistol in his hand, and calling out, "What happened?" He joined the group surrounding Veronica, then faced out toward the forest, ostentatiously keeping the pistol in front of himself as he scanned the terrain.

Over the radio, Dan could hear the team of sheriffs further up the trail, as they worked to search and clear the area. So far they had found nothing, and were now moving up the trail towards Monument Lake.

Dan realized that the slowest walker by far was Gloria. He looked at Luis and asked him, "Can you let Gloria ride your horse from here?"

A flicker of pain showed in Luis' face, but he quickly agreed. "Okay, we can do that. I'll just have to adjust the saddle."

Dan turned to the rest of the group. "So here's the plan. Gloria will ride down the trail with Luis in front. We're going to follow on foot—and we should be able to move pretty quickly this way. We've got about a mile of steep downhill here, and then the trail flattens out."

He turned to Ralph Gephart. "Ralph, the way Sheriff Healey set it up before, he took the last spot, and watched our backs. If you do that, I'll lead the hikers, and we'll just try to get out of here as quickly as possible."

Ralph considered this carefully. He slowly eased his way back to the end of the line, eyes never ceasing to search the woods.

Luis finished adjusting the saddle, and what followed was a titanic struggle to get Gloria up onto the horse. She could not lift herself into the saddle, not even with Luis giving her an energetic helping hand. After three attempts, Gloria refused to try again.

Luis then spotted a rock further down the trail, and with some help they positioned Gloria on top of it, Veronica and Kristen holding her hands to help balance her. Luis led the horse up to her, and they tried again. This time both Luke and Peter had to lend a hand, hoisting and heaving the heavy woman onto the saddle. In so doing, they very nearly shoved her over the horse and off the other side.

Gloria yelled and grabbed onto the saddle horn with both hands, her legs on one side of the horse, and her head hanging down on the other. Only Luis, with his experience, was able to grab her left leg and hold on. Slowly Gloria worked her right leg into position, grunting and complaining as she did so. Finally she was seated atop the horse, and the parade could begin.

Luis led his horse down the trail, and the pack train followed him. Dan waited just long enough for a bit of the dust to settle, then waved the rest of the family to follow him. As they did so, he could see Ralph in the rear, with his pistol in his hand. His head was swiveling from one side to the other, keeping a careful watch on the woods.

Once through the switchbacks and down into the flatter section of the trail, Dan checked his watch again. With two miles to go, it would take them only an hour to get to the trailhead. And with each step he grew more confident that the danger was past.

Adding to this confidence was the sound of a helicopter overhead. Cal had called in the chopper to assist in searching the area around the lake, and they had flown in the SAR team as well, to recover

Rafael's body from the lake. Apparently the situation was serious enough that they were willing to use the chopper, even though that was rarely done in a designated wilderness.

Dan couldn't argue with the decision. As far as he knew, the Himmel family was the only group with a permit for Monument Lake, and they were certainly not going to complain—at least not about the helicopter.

The family was beginning to show signs that they were more at ease as well. Luke and Peter began a conversation about what they were going to eat once they got into town, and by the time they reached the trailhead, every member of the family had expressed an opinion. Most had voted for a fat hamburger and beer, but Gabriela wanted a green salad and pizza.

Dan was glad that Gloria was too far ahead to participate in the conversation. He was sure she would have a hard time finding the perfect meal to meet her expectations in Sonora.

# chapter 28

The scene at the trailhead was chaotic.

Dan knew that there would be a group of people there, but the number of vehicles surprised even him. There were two California Highway Patrol cars, apparently to escort the group out once they were ready to leave. Through the trees another CHP car could be seen out on the main road, and it had blocked all traffic in to the trailhead. And there were two more officers from the Sheriff's Department directing people and traffic.

Monica Lawson was there, from the forest service. She, too, had worn her sidearm, Dan noted. By the time Dan walked in to the trailhead, she was helping Luis manage the process of getting Gloria down off the horse.

Additional vehicles from the officers up the trail were parked around the trailhead, along with the Himmel family vehicles, and three horse trailers.

As the hikers entered the trailhead, the two sheriffs were taking charge, trying to usher everyone into their squad cars.

Gabriela was not about to be bullied. "I am going to the restroom, and there is nothing you can do to stop me!" she yelled at one of the officers. He backed off and looked at Dan.

Dan held his hands up to show restraint, then joined the two sheriffs. Monica also came over to listen in on the conversation, as did Ralph Gephart.

"We're supposed to take them all directly into town," explained the object of Gabriela's anger. "They want to get these people into the station and make sure they are safe, and get their statements as well."

"I think we're better off explaining that to them," Dan said. "Let's let everybody catch their breath and maybe get a drink, and then we'll explain what the plan is."

Ralph interrupted to ask, "Are we going to keep them separated, so they don't have a chance to talk to each other?"

The second sheriff looked at him quizzically. "Are these suspects? I thought we were trying to get them out of here because they were victims..."

"That's right," Dan agreed. "I can take a couple of people in my car, and maybe Monica can take another three people in hers?" He looked at Monica, who nodded in agreement. "I think they might prefer to be in the Forest Service trucks instead of the sheriff's cars. And then you guys bracket us on the road?"

"Sure," replied the deputy. "We've got a CHP officer in front, and one in the back. And Larry and I will follow them. You two will be in the middle with the family."

Dan looked at Monica again. "Why don't you take the women, and I'll take the men?" He felt slightly guilty at foisting Gabriela on the younger ranger, but he also knew that it would reduce tensions if she would agree.

"Sure," said Monica. "And what about Kristen?"

"I can take her in my car," Ralph offered.

A twinge went through Dan, but he knew it made no sense to argue. He wanted to warn Monica about Gabriela. "She's very tough, very aggressive," he said. "Just explain that you are following your orders, and your first priority is to make sure they are safe."

Monica nodded.

By this time the family had emerged, and Kristen and one of the sheriffs had suggested they all drink some water. Dan explained the plan to them and was completely surprised to hear no protests from the Himmel family.

He led Peter and Luke to his truck, and the three men climbed in. The seat was blistering hot from the sun, and Peter in his shorts let out a shout of pain. Dan started up the truck and quickly switched on the air conditioning.

One by one the cars came to life, and slowly began to emerge out onto the road. Dan had never driven in this sort of caravan before, and was a bit amused as the CHP officers put on their flashing lights and led the way.

"Looks like we are going to get the royal treatment," he said to Luke and Peter.

"I guess we're not trying to sneak into town, huh?" Luke asked.

"At this point, what we're trying to do is get you somewhere safe until we can figure out what's going on," Dan replied.

He checked his rear-view mirror. Behind him, Kristen sat next to Ralph in his F-150. They didn't seem to be having much of a conversation.

The cars rolled through the mountain roads, dipping into one canyon and then climbing back out onto yet another ridge. Sunlight fell on the road in bars of white light between the trees.

It was a drive that Dan usually enjoyed, often taking time to look for wildlife as he drove along. Just last week he had seen a bear wandering through a clearing just below the road along here somewhere. But not today.

His thoughts drifted back up to Monument Lake, and what Cal Healey and his team might find up there.

# chapter 29

If they were planning to make a quiet entrance into Sonora, that wasn't going to happen. At the stoplight below Twain Harte the first CHP car started up its siren, and they rolled through every intersection looking for all the world like a presidential limousine parade. By the time they got to Sonora, Dan felt sure that most of the residents of Tuolumne County had either seen them pass by or heard about it from someone who had.

"Looks like you guys are getting the VIP treatment all the way," Dan said to his passengers.

Luke wasn't impressed. "If the goal is to make sure nobody knows where we are, then it would seem that the sheriff is new at this game. This is ridiculous."

"I think they just want to make sure that we all stick together," Dan explained. "There's no other way to make sure that we all go through the traffic lights together."

"Should we be waving at people?" Peter asked dryly. "I can't imagine this happens very often in this town."

The line of cars pulled up in front of the Sheriff's office, only to be met by more officers, at least two more from both the CHP and the Sheriff's Department. Peter Himmel chuckled. "Man, these guys must be loving the overtime for this," he said.

But once they got out of the truck, the two brothers were quickly hustled away into interview rooms, and within a couple of minutes Dan was surprised to look around and realize that except for the extra cars in the parking lot, there was no sign of who might be inside the building.

"That was quick!" he said to Monica, who had joined him outside on the sidewalk.

Ralph Gephart overheard the comment and responded. "They wanted to get everybody inside and into interview rooms as quickly as possible," he said. "And I guess they called to have some private security coming up to help."

Monica nodded. "Gabriela Himmel did that. She said she didn't want to leave it up to a couple of local yokel sheriffs."

Dan shook his head. "I bet that went over big."

Yet another sheriff's officer came out of the building and approached them. He studied them for a minute and then said to Dan, "Are you Courtwright?"

Dan nodded.

"They want you inside," he said. To the other two rangers he said, "Unless you guys learned something on the ride over here, you can take off. We'll be doing the de-briefings here, and we'll keep you posted on anything we get."

Ralph was clearly uncomfortable with this. "This happened in a National Forest, and it's our jurisdiction," he said. "I can't abandon the scene unless I am directed to by my superior."

The sheriff waved his arm in dismissal. "You can do whatever you want. Check with your office. They've turned the case over to us, and you're welcome to help out—but you may have to do it on your own time. It's our case."

He and Dan started to walk back inside the building. As they stopped just outside the door, he asked Dan, "So you were up at Monument Lake when all this happened?"

"Yeah," Dan replied. "I was the one who made the first call. Cal Healey got up there a few hours later. That was yesterday... seems like a long time ago."

"Well, they're going to want to get a statement from you," the sheriff explained, opening the door for the ranger.

"I've got it all in my notes," Dan said as he walked through the door.

Dan was led into a small office and invited to sit down. "We'll get someone here to talk with you right away," said the sheriff. "Do you want some coffee? Water? Soda?"

Dan looked at his watch: 12:45. "No, thanks... well, maybe some water. What I would really like is some lunch," he said with a half-smile.

The sheriff nodded and walked out of the office.

Dan looked around the office and was grateful that his job didn't require him to spend much time in a place like this. Clearly designed and built in the 1980s, the place was dreadfully tired and impersonal. It occurred to Dan that you could take this office and put it anywhere in the world, and people would recognize it for what it was: a small office of a petty administrative official.

A middle-aged and overweight secretary came into the office and said, "Are you Dan Courtwright?" When Dan admitted to this fact, she pointed to the phone. "You have a call on line two."

Dan picked up the phone. It was his boss, Steve Matson. "Hi, Dan. Heard you had quite an adventure up there this week."

"Hi, Steve. What's up?" Dan answered.

"What were there? Two deaths? And a shooter? Are you okay?" Matson asked.

"I'm fine. A little hungry, but fine."

"Good. Listen, Dan." Steve was now going to ask for a favor. Dan could tell by the way he started the sentence; he had worked for Matson long enough to know this pattern. "We're pretty under-staffed right now. I think you know that. And this case is going to use up a lot of people. I just don't think that we have the resources right now to take this on. Do you?"

Dan blew a small amount of air our between his lips before answering. "Nope, I don't."

"So I've asked the Sheriff to take this over," continued Matson. "Is that okay with you?"

"Steve, you know this isn't my favorite part of the job," Dan replied. "If you want to turn this over to them, I'm just fine with that."

"Great," Steve responded, and by the way he did it, Dan knew that there was more to come. "That's great. And they are going to need a li-aison with us… somebody they can work with as they move forward." Steve paused here, waiting for a response from Dan. He got none. "I've suggested that you might be the best person to do that."

Dan thought about this. Apparently, he thought about it too long, be-cause Steve Matson then spoke again. "I just think you're the best guy, Dan. You were there, you know the area, and you've spent some time with the people…."

Dan continued to think it over, and then responded, "Yeah." It wasn't clear if he was accepting the assignment, or just agreeing with the facts.

Matson interpreted it as the latter. "Thanks, Dan. I know you have a couple of days off coming…."

"Yeah…" Dan replied.

"If you can, I'd like to ask you to take those later, so that you can stay on this for a few days right now. Maybe take this afternoon off? But they're going to organize a major search up there tomorrow, and I'd really like you to be there for that. Will that work for you? I'll make it up to you, I promise."

Dan knew that for all of Steve's other idiosyncrasies, he really did keep his word when it came to staff time and schedules.

"Yeah, okay. I can do that," Dan replied with a sigh.

"Thanks, Dan. Now go home and get some rest." Steve hung up the phone.

Dan hung up the phone and put his hands behind his head. He leaned back in his chair and gave a huge sigh.

He was still sitting in that position three minutes later when yet another sheriff walked into the office.

"You Dan Courtwright?" the sheriff asked.

Dan sat forward and said, "Yep, that's me."

The sheriff grinned. "I've got twenty bucks for a Mexican restaurant, a couple of beers, and a chance to talk over your notes with you."

"That sounds terrific," Dan said with enthusiasm. His stomach growled as he stood up to follow the deputy out the door.

# chapter 30

The tortilla chips were lousy. Yes, they were home-made, but that didn't make them good. Too thick and heavy, too greasy, not enough salt. Dan finished every chip in the basket in three and a half minutes. By the time the waitress came back with their beers, the basket was empty, and Deputy Larry Maguire was chuckling.

"How long were you out this time?" he asked Dan.

Dan had to think about the answer. The complications of the last two days had made him lose count. "Five or six days… something like that."

The beers arrived and Larry hoisted his glass toward Dan. "Well, here's to having you back," he said.

Dan took a swallow of beer and closed his eyes, concentrating on the pleasure the cold drink provided his palate. After a moment of reflection, he opened his eyes and saw Larry staring at him. "Man, that tastes good," Dan said.

Larry decided that it was time to get down to business. "So talk me through what happened up there," he said. "You were up above Monument Lake?"

And so Dan related his story. When the food arrived, Larry suggested that they just go ahead and eat. "We've got plenty of time," he said. "Enjoy the food, and we'll get back to this when we're done eating."

Dan didn't argue, but he did pull out his notes and scanned them for details, chewing all the time. He appreciated Larry's thought, but Dan didn't want to spend all afternoon in Don Manolo's Mexican Fine Food. He wanted to get back to his house and take a shower.

As he mopped up the last of his sauce from his chiles rellenos, Dan looked up to see with surprise that Larry was only half-through with his lunch. Larry met his gaze and asked, "Good?"

Dan nodded with a grin. "I think I needed that."

"Okay," Larry replied, "so why don't you work through your notes and just give me everything you've got. I have a recorder here and I'll have one of the secretaries get it all transcribed by tonight."

Dan picked up the story and filled Larry in as best he could.

Dan was surprised about how many details he could recall, and by the time he had finished, he felt thoroughly drained. He'd been talking pretty much non-stop for an hour and fifteen minutes. As he wrapped up the story, Dan sat back and looked at Larry, who had been taking notes while Dan talked.

"Okay," Larry said, sitting forward. "Let me ask you a few things now, to fill in the details." He paused to look at his notes. "I think one of the things we'd like to do is to get a topo map of the area, and have you chart where each person was during this time. Maybe track them, hour by hour, so that we can get a sense of who was where, and who might have seen what. Can you help with that?"

Dan nodded, but the look on his face clearly betrayed his feelings.

"We don't have to do that today," Larry reassured him. "I'll get it started with our staff, and maybe sometime in the next couple of days you can fill in some of the details."

"Sure," Dan replied, his body language obviously communicating the relief he felt at this news.

"Good," Larry continued. "And then I think we have a clear picture of where everyone was yesterday morning, when Max Himmel died..." He scanned his notes again. "But what we don't have is a good idea of where these people were later on in the evening. That's when Rafael died... can you pinpoint where everyone was?"

Dan thought about this for a moment. "Kristen Gallagher was making dinner for everyone—she's the cook, from over in Twain Harte. I know about her." He paused again and thought. "I think Gabriela was in her tent on the radio." He looked at Larry. "She had a full communications setup in there—not exactly the wilderness experience..."

"Did you see her in the tent?" Larry asked.

"No... I don't remember. I think I heard her in there." Dan was suddenly confused. "I'm sorry, I was so focused on trying to figure out what happened that morning that I really wasn't paying much attention in the afternoon." He tried to organize his thoughts for the deputy. "We had the SAR team there in the morning, and Cal was over with them. By the time he returned...we set up our tent...."

Dan fell silent as he tried to sift through the details in his mind.

Larry sat back and waited. "Take your time," he said, "but it's better if we try to capture all this now, rather than have you sleep on it..."

"Yeah, I know," said Dan. "I know all the women were in camp at one point, but then Gloria and Veronica left for a bit, and Peter went for a swim... maybe about 5:00 or so? Washed all that dust and chalk off. And Luke was... I don't remember seeing where Luke was until right at dinner time. And Rafael was fishing—probably illegally by then."

Larry looked at him quizzically.

"He was catching fish for everyone for dinner. When we found his creel later that night, it had more than his five fish limit," Dan explained.

"And after dinner, we were all in camp for a while, except for Rafael," Dan continued. He told Larry about the inflatable doll in the sleeping bag, and the moonlight search of the lake. It seemed so long ago to Dan now.

Dan realized how tired he was, and how confused his words must sound to the deputy. "I'm sorry, this isn't very helpful." Dan was embarrassed at his inability to give Maguire better information.

"Don't worry," the deputy responded. "We'll get a statement from each of the family members as well, and from Kristen. It's just a good idea to try to get all this down first, before we start asking you to corroborate something they might say."

Dan nodded.

"And Cal will be here later today," Larry said. "They're flying him out with the body on the SAR chopper. So we'll get his statement as well."

"I'm sure that will help you more than I did," Dan replied.

"Yeah, maybe…" Larry was still checking his notes. "One more thing, Dan. When you guys were on the trail out… and you stopped for a break?"

"Yeah," Dan remembered. "There was a bit of a false alarm about my pack there on the trail, but Gloria insisted we stop for her to go 'find a bush.' So we did. Cal was there, and he agreed…."

"And Peter gets shot?" Larry encouraged him.

"The women were up on one side of the trail. Cal was keeping watch there. And Peter just walked right around to the other side of a couple of big firs right there on the trail. Ten, fifteen seconds later, Peter comes running back saying that the tree exploded, and he's dripping blood from his ear. Something slashed a line right through the side of his ear…"

"How loud was the report? What kind of gun do you think it was? Could you tell?" Larry asked.

Dan shook his head. "I couldn't tell. There was some kind of loud bang. Not like a big caliber gun. Something small? But there was a lot going on right then. And it seemed like somebody sneezed…" He paused here. "I think Cal thought that maybe it was somebody with a silencer—at least to reduce the noise some."

Larry looked at him in surprise.

"These people have made some real enemies," Dan responded. "And from what we learned the night before, and then when Cal found Rafael, we figured this could be a serial killer... maybe a professional. That's why we wanted to get them out of there."

Larry thought this over and looked back at his notes, then looked back at Dan. "But if the shooter had a gun, why wouldn't he have just shot them all, one by one, as they wandered around the lake?"

Dan held up his hands as if to fend off an attack. "Hey, I don't know who this is, and I don't know their motivations. Don't ask me to explain their methods!"

Larry sat across from him chewing quietly on his cheek as he studied the notes he had taken. "Fair enough," he said to Dan. He turned to wave to the waitress and request the bill. "And you don't need to hang around here for now. Go home, get a shower, and get some rest. I understand that they want you to join the group that's heading up there again tomorrow?"

"That's what I heard," Dan said.

Larry gave Dan his business card. "Give me a call later this evening, and I'll be able to tell you if we've learned anything more... or just check with Cal. I'll make sure he's in the loop. Does that work for you?"

"Yeah, that's great," Dan said. He couldn't keep the exhaustion from creeping into his voice.

Larry gave him a sympathetic smile. "Go home, get some rest," he said, and patted him on the shoulder.

Dan walked out of the restaurant into the heat of the afternoon. His truck would be hotter than hell now. He opened the door to let some of the heat out, then decided that it just didn't matter anymore. He got in, started the motor, turned the A/C up to maximum, and headed for home.

# chapter 31

By the time Dan pulled his truck in front of his house, the air conditioning had finally brought the brutal heat back into moderation, which just meant that his sweaty body was now starting to feel the chill. Added to his week in the back country, it made Dan want to head straight for the shower.

He peeked inside the mailbox on the porch of his little bungalow cabin, but he knew there would be nothing inside. Pat and Walt, the retired couple next door, would have already collected the mail and placed it on his dining room table.

He unlocked the door and walked over to the table. The basket was overflowing with a pile of catalogs, junk mail, and bills. He flipped through them quickly, identifying a few that would bear further investigation. A few of the catalogs went into a stack for late night musings, and the rest were left on the table. He'd toss it all later.

A quick check of the phone messages showed only four calls. He punched the button to listen to them while he unbuttoned his shirt and peeled it off. The first was a blank message; someone had hung up on the machine. By the time he bent over to untie his boots, the second message came on, this one from a political candidate who wanted his support. He pulled off the boot and hit the machine to skip to the next message: another blank one. Dan pulled the sock off his right foot.

He was always surprised at how dirty his feet became on the trail. Even though he washed his feet every night, the dirt just built into huge dark splotches on his ankles and feet. The last and latest message must have come in the last few minutes. A sheriff dispatcher had called to tell him that Cal Healey had Dan's backpack, and would drop it by later this evening when Cal got back from Monument Lake.

Dan slipped off his pants and underwear, and collected all his clothes in his arms, leaving the boots by the telephone. Stark naked, he carried the clothes into the laundry room and tossed them directly into the washing machine. He didn't start the machine because it would have made taking a shower unbearable. In the old section of town, the water pressure was so low that he would alternately boil and freeze in the shower as the washing machine made its demands on the water supply.

He walked into the bathroom and turned on the shower full blast. While he waited for the water to get warm, he looked into the mirror, and was surprised to see that he didn't look nearly as dirty as he felt. Yes, the beard was unkempt and his hair was flattened on his head, but he still recognized himself. He ran his hand over his face and felt the sticky film of dirt and sweat rub off on his fingers.

Steam began to drift out of the shower, and Dan opened the door and stepped in. He gave a huge sigh as he felt the warm water wash over him, then stuck his head directly in the spray and let it pound on his head. It didn't take him long to wash his body and shampoo his hair. It took longer for the ache of the trail to wash off. Bit by bit Dan began to feel refreshed. He let the spray hit one part of his body, then another, and allowed his mind to drift. He slowly changed the water temperature from steaming to almost cool, took one more long stretch directly under the spray, then turned the shower off and reached for a towel.

Once he had dried himself off, Dan wrapped the towel loosely around his waist and went to turn on his computer. He scanned the new email messages, opened one from his sister and another that looked like it might be from his bank, and then opened up his web browser. It was time to learn a little more about the Himmel family.

A quick Google search revealed more information than he ever expected. The most complete information seemed to come from the website of the Himmel Glass Factory. In addition to information about the glasses ("The best wine glass, every time"), Dan found a summary of Max Himmel's life story—a meteoric rise to his position as one of the most powerful and influential men in the German economy.

Max Himmel was a legendary businessman, a self-made man whose family had been quite wealthy before World War II. His father was an industrialist and a famous gourmet, with a world class wine cellar. They lost everything in the War, and Max began working as a shoe-shine boy in the Frankfurt train station. From there he worked himself up to a waiter in the station restaurant. That launched him on his path. His education and bearing impressed customers, and his experience with wine and food helped him become a well-known sommelier within a few years. He moved to New York, where he managed to find a job at one of the top restaurants in Manhattan, and within a few years he had opened his own wine shop next door to Grand Central Station. The shop became a huge success and every wine lover who traveled soon learned to stop in his shop to taste the latest releases and learn the most recent gossip about the world of wine.

He was frustrated with the kinds of wine glasses available for his customers, and he offered to design a better glass for one of his German suppliers. The new glasses, with a larger bowl and longer stem, quickly became the rage, and Max soon bought out his partner and became owner of the glass factory. From that point on, according to the website, the story was one of continued successes. New designs, new glasses, and a virtual domination of the world of fine wine glasses. By the late 1990s he had bought out almost every competitor, and his empire had expanded well beyond wine glasses. He had a crystal mine in

Austria, a huge tract of timber in Patagonia, a winery and wine barrel company in Hungary, and a winery supply company that sold corks, capsules, and laboratory and filtration equipment to major wineries on three continents. And he had played important roles in the re-birth of Eastern Europe, as well as the stock market in Germany. He was the largest wine distributor in Russia.

Dan was impressed. It seemed as if everything that Max Himmel touched was destined for international success. He had married Cristiana, a devout Catholic girl from a small town near Munich, in 1958. The couple had seven children, and all of them, according to the website, were highly successful in their own fields. There was a short profile on each one of them, but those didn't offer Dan anything he didn't already know.

Looking for more depth, Dan then started searching for news stories about the family. Almost immediately he found estimates of the family's wealth that ranged from $250 million to nearly $500 million. But he also noted a number of stories about the business dealings of Max Himmel: he spent a lot of time in court. Sometimes he sued other people; sometimes other people sued him. As Dan checked into the news coverage of almost every single Himmel business, he found lawsuits. Max's first partner in the wine shop had sued him and lost everything. The first glass company had to declare bankruptcy, and Max then purchased it from the court for pennies on the dollar. The crystal mine changed hands when Max called in a debt from a family friend who was struggling financially.

In Chile, there was an outcry because the timber company and its 400,000 acres of wilderness had been paid for with funds that were technically frozen after World War II. When the sale was finally approved by the Chilean court, the seller, the stately old Forlan family from Santiago, received only forty percent of the expected price. The judge in the case later purchased a portion of the property from

Max, and the Chilean press suggested that it was a payoff. The Forlans complained bitterly and publicly about the situation, but the rise of Allende in Chile led them to leave the country. They now lived in Venezuela in greatly reduced circumstances, and the father committed suicide in 1994.

The winery supply company began with Himmel distributing corks to wineries, but when the wineries sued him for delivering tainted corks that ruined their wine, Himmel was able to turn the case into a crusade against his Portuguese supplier. By the time the case was resolved he owned both the cork company and seventeen hundred hectares of cork forest in the Alentejo that had been in the Soares family for nearly four hundred years.

The Hungarian barrel company was started within weeks of the fall of the iron curtain. While others struggled to find ways to move forward during this very complicated transition period, Max Himmel seemed to have had no difficulties at all. There were some reports that he had used secret police connections in the former Soviet Union to grease the skids, and reports that his wine distribution system was heavily involved in laundering money in Russia. Dan had heard about doing business in Russia and could only imagine what kind of deals had been made.

At every turn, Max Himmel had entered into every battle, and he had won just about every time. Dan could only imagine some of the enemies he had made in the process.

Dan changed directions and started a search for each one of Max Himmel's children.

# chapter 32

Peter Himmel had his own website, complete with photos of himself on top of Mount Everest, and a long list of great climbs he had personally led to success. It was an impressive list, but Dan noted that the most recent climb was now six years ago, and the website itself seemed to be a few years out of date.

The site was filled with quotes from great climbers through the ages, and challenged its visitors to "accept the challenge of reaching the top!" for whatever peak or route they wanted to climb. As Dan scanned the site, he recognized some of the top climbers in the world who had teamed up with Peter Himmel on adventure after adventure. While there were the usual ascents of granite faces in Yosemite, many of the longer expeditions were in the Andes, where Himmel offered "unique opportunities to reach some of the most challenging summits in the world." And the base camp for these adventures was the Himmels' Punto del Cielo estate in Chilean Patagonia.

The photos of the estate were stunning: towering peaks, glaciers clinging to near-vertical faces, rock and snow reflected in the mirrorlike waters of blue-black lakes. And Dan noted something else as well: in every one of these photos, Peter was grinning—not just smiling, but grinning from ear to ear. Grinning, as Dan's grandmother used to say, like a first-class fool.

There was controversy here as well. During one of Peter's climbs of Cerro del Aguila there had been a tragic accident. Hope Harrison, an American woman hoping to be the first woman to scale the Culo del Diablo route, had fallen a hundred and fifty feet down the mountain. Peter Himmel had rappelled down to her, and claimed that he had found her dead. He came down the mountain and organized a mission to recover her body. But when they arrived, his lead climber had discovered a note she had written after Peter left her. The note did not blame Peter Himmel, and many climbers noted that there was no difference between a rescue and a recovery in that situation—both would have arrived at the same time, with the same results. But Hope's family was outraged, and sued Peter Himmel for millions of dollars. The case was settled out of court, and the authorities had declined to press any charges against Peter Himmel.

When Dan dug deeper into more recent news stories, he learned that Peter was no longer based in Patagonia, but had been called back to run the family businesses in Europe. The stories quoted Max Himmel as being delighted that Peter had done so well, and that this experience would give him an even better perspective on achieving the goals they had for their European holdings.

But a story in a climbers' magazine had an interview with Peter just two months before the change. Peter swore that he would never leave Patagonia, and that he would happily give up his role in business to stay there. As a part of the story, some of his climbing colleagues were asked to give their opinion of Peter. Perhaps the best quote came from Marshall Follett, who said, "His family may be wealthy, but Peter doesn't give a damn about money. For him, it's all about being on the mountain. No more, no less."

Dan couldn't help wondering what had made Peter change his mind. He spent a few minutes trying to find something more, but failed. It was as if Peter Himmel the climber had simply disappeared, and Dan could not bring him back to life. After a few more minutes of fruitless clicking through websites, he turned his attention to Luke.

There seemed to be less hard information about Luke Himmel. Dan found a few mentions of his name in stories about the Himmel family, but Luke seemed to be involved at a reduced level compared to Peter, Gabriela, and Gloria. After a while, Dan began to play with variations on the search words for Luke, hoping somehow to separate Luke from his more visible siblings. It was only on the fourth try that Dan found some new listings, and three of them were in Spanish. It took Dan a few minutes to work through the internet translation of the stories, but when he did a rather disturbing pattern emerged.

Luke was named in two different paternity suits in Latin America; one in Brazil and one in Argentina. And there had been quite a scene in a restaurant in Buenos Aires when the family of one of the women, who appeared to be only eighteen at the time, confronted Luke in the restaurant and the altercation led to the arrival of the police.

On the fourth page of the search, there was a note about charges filed against Luke for sexual harassment in New York seven years ago. The story said that he had been accused, and charges filed, but Dan could find no further mention of the case in any other search. He assumed that it had been settled out of court.

On a hunch, he checked the national sex offender database. And there he was. His photo wasn't quite as glamorous as Dan remembered him, but he was there. Along with all the usual information about Luke, there was a single listing, from eleven years ago, that said his victim had been a fourteen-year-old girl in Denton, Texas.

Dan sat back in his chair and took a deep breath. A heavy, dreary cloud of disgust closed in around him. What had seemed like a good idea, searching out information about the Himmels, had only depressed him.

He glanced out the window and noted that it was now getting late in the day, and the last hour of sunlight was adding its warmth to the trees in the yard. He knew he should probably go out there and check on his garden. Some of the tomatoes must certainly be getting ripe by now, and the bonsai maple could use a few well-chosen snips on the ends of its branches.

And still he sat in the chair. He would have liked to talk with someone. He thought of calling his sister, Naomi, but he knew that the conversation would not give him comfort. Naomi had problems of her own, and he didn't feel like hearing them today.

He slowly got up from the computer and walked over to the sofa, first sitting down in the middle of it to thumb through a magazine, then stretching out on it full length, and putting his right arm over his eyes. He propped his feet up on the armrest on the far end and allowed himself to drift off into sleep.

# chapter 33

Dan drifted in his sleep, slowly floating above Monument Lake. As he looked down into the lake, he realized that he could see deep into the water. There were logs there, and he could see the white of the granite ridges in the bottom as well. Dan wondered if Rafael could see the fish in this lake. Dan couldn't see Rafael's body anywhere. They must have already removed it. And then he was drifting over to the campsite.

He could see the Himmel family there, and Kristen, too. But something was wrong. They were all cowering behind logs and rocks, keeping watch on the forest around them. Dan couldn't see into the forest from his perspective above the campsite, and he wanted to do something to help them.

Dan allowed himself to drift over the trees, hoping to help them find their attacker. But one of the trees was too tall, and he floated into it. He could hear his body slowly banging into the tree, and yet he couldn't get past it.

He woke up suddenly, realizing that someone was knocking on his front door.

With a pang of regret that his delicious nap was over, he swung his legs off the sofa, pulled on a pair of pants, and walked to the front door. Through the frosted glass he could see that the person outside was leaving, walking off the porch and back to the street.

Dan opened the door and Cal Healey turned around, carrying Dan's backpack over one shoulder.

"Sorry," Dan apologized. "I was just napping on the sofa."

"Hey—I'm the one who should apologize," Cal said. "I hate disturbing anyone who has the time to take a nap!"

Dan smiled. "It's been a long couple of days…" he admitted.

"It sure has," Cal agreed. "I thought you might want your backpack. I guess when you left it you had other things on your mind." Cal handed the backpack to Dan, who left it on the floor of the porch.

"No kidding," Dan replied. "But hey—we managed to get everyone back to town safely. I guess you know that?"

Cal nodded. "The whole family is at the Sugar Pine Motel. I don't think that's the kind of accommodations they're used to, but that's all we've got. We've got a couple of deputies there, and get this: they've got a bunch of security guards on their way as well." He paused to think about this. "I can't really blame them, I guess, but the Sugar Pine has never been so protected!"

Dan could only imagine what the little motel looked like with all this attention. "Did you find anything up at the lake?" Dan asked Cal.

"Not really," Cal said slowly. "There's a lot of territory up there. We did what we could, but we didn't really find anything. Our biggest concern was making sure the area was secure, and I think we did that. We'll go back tomorrow to do a more thorough search for evidence."

"I guess I'm supposed to join you for that," Dan noted.

"Well, we can use all the help we can get up there. We're going to have about fifteen guys up there."

"So do we know any more than we did when I left you?" Dan asked.

"We're still talking to everyone in the family," Cal answered. He thought about it for a moment. "That's quite a family, you know."

"I know" said Dan. "I did a little checking on the internet. They've got a lot of fingers in a lot of pies." And Dan proceeded to share much of what he had seen on his Google searches for information about the Himmels.

"Oh, it's better than that," Cal responded. "When we talked to these guys, every one of them swears that he has no enemies, and that he can't imagine who would want to do something like this. But every one of them then goes on to say that Peter, or Gloria, or Max, now that's another story. Swear to God, every one of these people says that they are as pure as driven snow, but that just about every one of their brothers and sisters has done something that has made them an enemy for life. Sometimes two or three times."

"Wow…" Dan mulled this over. "That's a lot of stuff to track down."

"No kidding," Cal agreed. "We don't get a lot of murders up here, and when we do, most of them are pretty simple cases of somebody getting too drunk or too angry and killing their wife or brother or something. This one's different. We have way too many potential suspects."

The word "murder" caught Dan's attention. "Did you get the autopsy reports?" he asked.

Cal nodded. "You already know about Max. He was killed by a rock in the back of the head. We don't have a full report on Rafael, but the doc did note that his neck is broken. That's pretty unlikely to be an accident. So we're working on the hypothesis that this is two murders… just the way you and I had it figured."

Dan took a deep breath and thought this over. "So we have a ton of potential suspects… but do we know if any of them are in the area?"

"Yeah, well… that's a bit of a problem." Cal looked at Dan. "You guys don't really get a lot of information on those permits you give out, do you?"

"Not really," Dan admitted. "We just ask people to fill in their names and addresses, and then we try to get them to give us a rough itinerary. It's really not about making them prove who they are—it's just about trying to find out where they are going, so if we have to look for them, we know where to start."

"We're trying to check about twenty permits you guys have issued. But the people who filed for the permits aren't home; they're somewhere up in the wilderness. And that's assuming that they are who they say they are. Two of the permits gave us addresses that don't match with anything. One isn't even a real street address."

Dan didn't like to think about the kinds of changes in paperwork that this case might cause for all the wilderness offices in the Sierra. For the second time today, he felt a wave of depression settle over him.

"But that's only the people who got permits," Cal continued. "Who knows how many other people are up there without getting a permit?"

"Yeah, that's always a problem," Dan admitted.

"So anyway, we're all meeting at the trailhead at 6:30 tomorrow morning," Cal told him.

"Okay, I'll make it there." Dan replied. He looked down at his backpack. Tonight he would throw all the clothes in the washing machine and try to air out his sleeping bag and tent. He picked up the pack by the loop on the top. It seemed heavier than he remembered.

"Hey, listen…" Cal began. "I don't know if you have any plans for dinner," he said as he looked past Dan into the bungalow, "but you're welcome to join us. Maggie is just making some hamburgers and things, but there's plenty of food for you."

"Thanks," Dan answered, "but I think I'll stick around here and get a few things done. I've been gone for a while, and I want to make sure the place isn't falling apart."

"You got cold beer in the fridge?" Cal asked.

"Yeah," Dan laughed. "I do. Thanks."

Cal stuck out his hand to Dan. "See you tomorrow. That was good work up there today. Thanks."

"Ah hell, thank you," Dan replied. "You did the hard part."

"Nope," Cal replied. "You dealt with the family. All I had to do was look for a murderer."

The two men laughed, and Cal walked back to his car.

Dan hefted the pack over one shoulder and walked back into his house. It was time to see exactly what kind of beer he did have in his fridge.

# chapter 34

Dan was unprepared for the scene at the trailhead the next morning. For one thing, he couldn't find a place to park. The trailhead parking lot was not only full, but there were five or six vehicles out on the road. He took a look at the sun, tried to estimate where it would be in the afternoon, and then parked fifty feet further down the road, where he thought his truck might be shaded from the worst of the heat.

It was a game he played every time he parked in the mountains, and he was pretty good at it.

Dan didn't recognize some of the cars. There were Forest Service and sheriffs' cars, and at least three SAR trucks. In one corner of the lot he could see horse trailers as well. But many of the cars lacked the color schemes and logos Dan was accustomed to seeing on official vehicles. The only indications that they were part of the group were the small decals on the back window, or the government license plates they wore.

As he walked toward the trailhead parking lot, two men got out of such a car, wearing black jumpsuits with the letters FBI stenciled in white on the back. Dan wondered how those suits would feel as the men hiked up the trail. This morning wasn't too bad; the temperature was in the high sixties, and the sun was low enough to appear as streams of light between the trees. But this afternoon it would be a different matter. He didn't envy them.

At the trailhead, the large group was clustered around a picnic table by the outhouse. Dan quickly estimated six or seven sheriffs, two rangers like himself—was one of them Ralph Gephart? There were another half-dozen from local SAR teams, and more than that, maybe as many as a dozen FBI agents.

Standing on top of one of the tables was Sheriff Mark O'Malley. He was calling everyone to attention, and Dan hurried over to join the group. He got there just in time to hear O'Malley introduce the "man in charge of today's exercise," who worked for the FBI.

It was an impressive organization that they had put together, but then again, it was a complicated project. As the FBI agent explained, they were really doing two things at once. First of all, and most important, they were looking for a suspect who was armed, dangerous, and possibly hiding behind just about any tree.

As part of that search, they would not only use the mounted men to cover more ground, but they had three aircraft involved as well. There would be two helicopters searching the area near Monument Lake and the Valley above, and there would also be a CDF plane searching further afield, up in the high country. The helicopters would also take a crew of FBI agents into those areas, where they would begin to search on foot.

The second part of the search was going to focus on finding any evidence that might be in the area. That part of the search would be done on foot, and Cal Healey was brought to stand up on the picnic table to help organize that. Dan could see Cal wince just a bit from the pain in his knee as he climbed up on the table.

Cal began to give a brief description of the trail and the topography they could expect. When he saw Dan at the back of the group, he quickly pointed him out to the rest of the search team. "That's Ranger Dan Courtwright back there, and he knows this area better than anyone. He's the one who called this in originally. He and I will be coordinating efforts so that we can cover the ground as effectively as possible."

Dan felt the eyes of the group turn and look at him. He hoped they couldn't tell that Cal's praise had made him blush just a bit.

"Dan, I think I'll focus my group on the area just below the lake, where we were shot at yesterday," Cal explained. "And you can take your group up by the lake, to see what you can find around there."

Dan nodded in agreement.

The FBI agent took over again and started reading off the names of the people in each group. Dan tried to keep track of all the names and affiliations, but it was too much information all at once. He knew Larry Maguire would be with Cal's group, and that his group had only FBI agents in it. He was relieved to hear that Ralph was going to be in the CDF airplane, where he could direct the search pattern.

The meeting was breaking up, and Dan gathered his team near the trailhead itself. His group would leave first, since they had the farthest to travel. Cal's group would follow, and Dan couldn't help but think that Cal had arranged things that way to save his sore knee.

Dan looked over his group. There were seven serious FBI agents in front of him. "You guys know more about this than I do," he said, "so I am going to let you manage the search. But I will get you to where we are going… and that's about a two-hour hike. I'd really suggest that you have some extra water along. It's a dry trail." He pointed to the stack of supplies over by the restroom. "So grab a bottle and let's get going."

While Dan waited for the men to collect their water, he was surprised to see Peter Himmel walk down into the parking area, dressed in hiking boots, shorts, and a short-sleeved shirt. Peter had a brief discussion with Larry Maguire, who pointed in Dan's direction. Peter then walked over to Dan.

"I'd like to volunteer for this," Peter said to Dan.

Dan was dumbfounded. "I thought you were all under protection for now!" he said to Peter.

Peter ostentatiously looked around at the uniformed people in the parking lot. "Can you think of a safer place for me to be?" he asked. Then, in another tone of voice entirely, he spoke quietly to Dan. "Look, I've probably done more SAR missions than anyone here. I've got more certifications for this than anyone here. And I know these mountains. I know what do to."

Dan listened without giving any response. This was not a decision that he wanted to make.

"Besides," continued Peter, "this affects my family. For me, this is personal. I really want to help."

Dan sighed. Six FBI agents waited for him to make a decision. Dan looked at the nearest one and shrugged his shoulders. The agent shrugged in response.

"Okay," Dan sighed. "Stick with one of the agents here and stay in the group." He paused. "And if we hit any trouble at all, I want you all the way in the back."

"Sure," Peter replied. "And thanks."

With that, Dan led the group out on the trail up to Monument Lake.

# chapter 35

As soon as they hit the trail, Dan started having second thoughts about this group. While three of the agents were young and seemed to be in good shape, two of the older men were puffing hard within a few minutes. And one of the agents, in his mid-forties, was clearly suffering. This was on the flat section of the trail, where it followed an old jeep road for two miles along the valley floor. Once they reached the section that climbed the moraine up to the lake, it was going to be a struggle.

Dan wasn't completely unsympathetic to the laboring feds. After all, he sometimes led an occasional nature walk, and was used to taking his time, counting to twenty at every stop, and walking slower than he could possibly imagine, all to keep the group somewhat together.

But this wasn't a nature walk. He was anxious to get up to Monument Lake and get to work, and some of these guys were going to have a hard time with the pace. He slowed down a bit and tried to think of a slower-paced piece of music for his ear worm—a sedate adagio that would help him rein in his desire to march along the trail and leave the rest of the group behind.

It wasn't five minutes later that Peter Himmel tapped Dan on the shoulder and suggested that Dan stay with the slower hikers, while

Peter and the younger agents went ahead to get to work.

This struck Dan as a very bad idea, but it took him some time to think about why. "Peter, until we get up to the lake, and I can use the lay of the land to organize these guys, there is no point in getting up there. None of them have even seen this area before, and I want to make sure that we are all working as a team on this." Dan came to a stop and held his hand up when Peter started to interrupt him. "Those are the rules, Peter. If you don't like them, you can go back to the trailhead. And I have six FBI agents here who believe pretty strongly in doing this by the rules."

Peter gave a quick glance back at the men behind Dan and then nodded his agreement. To the nearest agent, a young African-American who had barely broken a sweat on the trail so far, Peter said, "I just want to get up there and get going. This is my family, and it's important to me."

"We'll get there," said the agent, whose name tag identified him as T. Parker.

Dan looked him over and was tempted to let him go ahead with Peter, if only to make the rest of the hike easier to manage.

Agent Parker pointed at Dan and said to Peter Himmel, "He's in charge, and we need all of these guys to do this right."

Peter looked from one to the other, searching for a face that would give him a more favorable response. Finding none, he nodded to Parker and waved the agent ahead of him on the trail.

As they walked, Dan could hear Peter muttering something under his breath, and didn't like the idea of a continuing stream of complaints as they hiked. But it was Parker who responded. "What's that? I didn't catch what you said," Parker said to Peter Himmel.

"Oh, nothing… nothing. I was just muttering…"

"I thought you said something about Veronica? Or Monica?" Parker asked him.

"No, no," Peter replied as they walked. After a few more steps he said, "I was just thinking that this is probably all because of Veronica's husband."

"How so?" Parker was now clearly operating as an FBI agent, rather than a fellow hiker. And he saw the opportunity to learn something as part of the conversation.

"Oh, it's nothing. But he's a banker in Turlock. That's a small town in the valley, and I know he's foreclosed on a lot of property down there."

"That's happening all over the country," one of the men further back in line suggested.

"Yeah," agreed Peter, "but Turlock isn't just some suburb... some of these guys are losing their family farms and things... and in the rest of the country, the banker isn't buying up a lot of the foreclosed properties for himself."

"Is that what he's doing?" asked Parker. "Seems like that would be hard to do... like there would be laws against it."

"He's not buying them up. Veronica is," Peter explained. "Through a holding company. But that can't be a secret in a small town like that. If somebody did that to me, and took my family farm, I'd be mad enough to do something violent about it."

Parker seemed to think this over before replying. "So why wouldn't somebody go for Veronica's husband first? Is he okay?"

"Oh, he's fine," said Peter, "but everybody in that town knows how he got his job, and why. It's our family money that did it. They know that. He's a small-time guy, and he and Veronica really aren't part of our family businesses. I mean, I know these are mortgages and things, but they are dealing with peanuts, and we deal in elephants."

The group hiked along in silence for a few moments while they thought this over.

It was Parker who continued the conversation. "So do you know if anyone has made any threats to them?"

"Yeah," Peter replied. "I heard Veronica telling Gabriela a couple of nights ago that they would have to slow down. Veronica was getting some pretty ugly phone calls, and she wanted Gabriela's advice. Gabriela told her to stop buying things until things cooled down."

"And did she?" asked Parker.

"That was just a couple of days ago, so it doesn't really matter... I think she agreed, but how would anybody in Turlock know that?" Peter answered.

"Yeah, I guess they wouldn't," agreed Parker.

Dan took a quick peek over his shoulder to see how the rest of the group was doing. The three slower agents were now about fifty feet behind them, but they didn't seem to be having any serious trouble with the pace. As so often happens on a hike, they had found their pace and a few people who were happy with it. And they were moving steadily, if slower than Dan and his group. Dan decided that he would keep up the current pace and get partway up the climb before he stopped and gave everyone a chance for water and a rest. In the meantime, Agent Parker could continue to chat with Peter Himmel.

"So Gabriela is the one she turns to for advice?" Parker asked Peter Himmel. "Gabriela is the one everyone asks for advice—if they want to make money," Peter answered. "She graduated summa cum laude in business and went straight to Wall Street. She made her own fortune in four years. She even started an investment firm while she was still in college. So when she got promoted to AVP at Morgan Stanley, that's when Dad called her and made her an offer she couldn't refuse. He said that anyone who could make more money than he could in the same time period deserved to run the whole show."

"So how did that sit with the rest of the kids?" asked Parker.

"Ah, hell, it was a foregone conclusion," said Peter. "Gabriela may have been the youngest, but she always won the Monopoly games as a kid, and she always insisted that she got to be the banker. It's who she is."

"Has she been successful?" asked Parker.

"Oh yeah," Peter answered. "She makes money when nobody else makes money." He paused, considering if he should say more. "She may not make friends, even in her own family, but she makes money like nobody else."

"And you guys are okay with that?" Parker asked.

Dan could hear a change in Peter's voice when he answered the question. Dan turned around to see that Peter had stopped on the trail, so that he could look at Parker in the face. "Look, our businesses are what let us live our lives," Peter said. "We have the lives we have because of those businesses, and Gabriela makes them all work. So we may not like some of the decisions, but we understand the system. And Gabriela makes it all work. So yeah, we're basically okay with that."

It didn't sound to Dan like a wholehearted endorsement of Gabriela Himmel's management style. He checked on the group behind and decided that it was time for a bit of water. Some of these guys in their black outfits were already looking hot and tired, and Dan needed them for the rest of the day. The one guy at the end of the line was decidedly red in the face.

# chapter 36

After the break, Dan led the group through an open forest, with some small meadows hidden among the trees. In the bright sunlight, it was almost as if they were outdoor stages, bright yellow and green, lit from above and ready for the actors to take their positions. But the trail soon reached the beginning of the moraine, and Dan could hear the stream off to his right, tumbling down the rocks noisily. From here, the net two miles would be uphill, with a series of switchbacks and steep inclines until they reached the lake.

He checked on the group behind him. Peter and Agent Parker were right with him, and two other agents were close behind. He could just see, through the trees, the last member of the team, working hard to keep in sight. He knew if he kept up his pace, he would lose them very quickly.

It took a conscious effort for Dan to slow down even more. Each footstep became a decision, and he gave himself plenty of time to breathe in time to this slower pace. He could feel the frustration build behind him, as Peter strained to keep himself in check. At one point, Peter actually stepped on Dan's heel, then muttered a quiet apology.

The trail staggered up a series of steep steps, nearly a foot high, and then shot up through a messy combination of cobble-sized stones and dirt. This was the kind of trail Dan liked least, and he could hear some of the others struggling with it as well.

He realized with a start that this section was where he had stopped just yesterday, and where Peter had run out of the forest with a wounded ear. He turned around and explained this to the rest of the group. "Please keep your eyes open along here," he continued. "We're actually supposed to go up by the lake, but if you see anything, let's not ignore it. This is all crime scene at this point."

The words not only served to give the agents warning; they also helped Dan justify the slower pace he had adopted.

"It seems like it was right over there," Peter Himmel said, as they walked along the trail, "behind those trees."

Dan could feel the attention of the group focus, and even their breathing seemed quieter as they walked up the trail through the trees.

"This is a hell of a place to try and find someone," Parker said.

Dan looked up to his right, where the stream cascaded down through dense alders, and manzanita bushes grew among the trees. As he came to the end of the first switchback, he heard something move in the bushes above him. He stopped and held up his hand... The rest of the group slowly came to a halt, one by one, as they noticed him stop.

Dan motioned for Parker to join him in the lead, and the two slowly crept up the trail towards the huge clouds of manzanita that grew at the end of the switchback. The bushes were more than head-high, and so dense that you could not see more than a couple of feet into them.

Agent Parker stepped forward, shielding Dan with his body, and raised his pistol, aiming it at the center of the bushes.

"FBI," he called out. "I need you to come out with your hands up."

Dan could hear other agents in the group begin to place themselves in position for a potentially dangerous situation, and he was grateful to have them with him.

Parker stepped slowly forward, glancing quickly back over his shoulder to see one of the agents step off the trail to the right and work into position there. Parker waved him forward, but the agent was having a tough time with the steep terrain below the trail. It was hard to focus on both the footing and the bushes.

Suddenly the bushes exploded, and they heard crashing noises as something large bolted out of the manzanita and broke off towards the stream at right.

The men instinctively dropped even lower in their stances and strained to see their adversary. Dan's heartbeat sped forward, suddenly throbbing in his ears.

It was Dan who first identified the large doe who leapt across an opening in the manzanita and raced across the stream, bounding up the hillside on the far side of the stream. Before he could say anything, one of the FBI agents behind called out, "It's a deer! Hold your fire!"

Parker turned around to Dan. "Let's not assume that there's nothing else here," he said. "I think we should check out the area and secure it."

"Well," Dan said, "I doubt that deer would have missed anything. If it is here, then I doubt there are any people nearby."

One of the agents called out from behind, "Is everybody good here?"

A chorus of assents were issued in response, and one of the agents said, "Yeah, but let's just get up to the lake and get to work."

"Hell, I have enough adrenaline right now, I could give that deer a run for its money," replied one of the others.

Parker turned to Dan. "Why don't you let me go first, and you right behind me?" he asked.

"No, that's all right," Dan replied, his heart still thrumming wildly in his chest. "I'll just take it slow, and if I see anything, I'll duck." He grinned at Parker.

"Duck fast," the agent replied with a smile.

From behind Dan heard more voices and conversation. He looked back to see Cal's team approaching them from below.

"You guys doing okay?" Cal called out.

"Oh yeah—just spooking a deer," Dan yelled back.

"That can be exciting," Cal said.

"It was," Dan agreed. He glanced at Peter Himmel, who seemed remarkably calm.

Peter noticed Dan looking at him. "Let's just get up there and get started," Peter said. "I want to get on with this."

# chapter 37

They stopped twice more before finally making it to the top of the moraine. Each time Dan called a halt and allowed the slower men to catch up, making sure that each one was drinking some water and not over-exerting himself. He began to feel a little like a den mother of a scout troop, but he also realized that these agents were not accustomed to either the elevation or the low humidity of the mountains. They were city boys, and he wanted to make sure that they didn't waste the whole day recovering from what was a fairly easy hike.

The stops also allowed the men to talk a bit more about what they were going to do at the lake, and about what they knew so far. Dan had to admit that Peter had been on his best behavior after the deer, simply hiking along in silence and staying happily in the middle of the faster group of hikers. And Agent Parker continued, in his own very low-key way, to pump Peter for more information.

During the first rest stop he had asked Peter about his other sister, the one that never came on these trips.

"That's Sophie," Peter explained. "She thinks we're all nuts."

"But she lives up here somewhere, doesn't she?" insisted Parker.

"Yep. She's sort of the reason we are all here," Peter said. "She moved here first, to Sonora, about fifteen years ago." Peter didn't seem to be interested in pursuing the subject, but Parker kept at it.

"So why did she move here?" he asked.

"Got me," shrugged Peter. "She said she liked the weather and the people. Mainly I think it was just to get away from the rest of us. She wanted a place that was so off the beaten track that none of us would want to follow."

"Did that work?" asked Parker.

Peter snorted. "It did for some of us. But she and Veronica are twins, so Veronica moved here with her husband, and got him a job over in Turlock."

"You seem to know these mountains pretty well..." Parker suggested.

"Well, I've done a bunch of climbing in Yosemite, so I've been through here a lot," Peter replied. "And it's not a very big place, so I know my way around... And then when Dad decided to start his mountain retreats, he figured that this was a good place to do it. He didn't want to give Sophie an excuse not to join us."

"Did she?" Parked asked.

"Never," Peter insisted. "She hated the whole idea of them. She said she just wanted to sit in her house and mind her own business, and not be any part of ours."

"So what is her business?" Parker asked Peter.

The question was met with a long silence, and Dan decided to help out. "She's some kind of artist, I think," he explained to Parker. "She's pretty famous around here for some of her stuff."

"She could be an artist, if she tried," said Peter, "but she doesn't. She thinks it's fun to see exactly how much people will pay for things that take absolutely no time or effort at all for her to create."

Parker looked at Dan, who shrugged his shoulders. "I've never seen much of her work," Dan explained. "I've just heard about it. And about the prices people pay for it."

Peter looked at Dan disdainfully. "People don't pay anything for it," he said. "She puts it up for auction, and Gabriela buys it. It's their little game. Gabriela buys it, and when she donates to museums, the donations always include something by Sophie… and an outrageous price attached to it. The only reason anyone else ever buys anything from Sophie is because they want to sell something to Gabriela."

Dan and Agent Parker looked at each other in surprise. "So you're saying that Gabriela supports Sophie?" Dan asked.

"From the beginning," Peter replied. "I don't think Dad ever figured it out. He was so proud of the fact that Sophie was not getting any of his money, because she wouldn't play his game. And I think he was even a little proud of Sophie for trying to make it on her own. But Gabriela had him completely fooled on that one."

Parker pushed Peter to explain more. "But didn't your dad notice the money? Or the museum stuff?"

"He never noticed, at least until this year," Peter said. "This year he asked about all the tax write-offs to the museums, and Gabriela promised him a full report later this year. But she's so good; she can hide anything she wants, and make it stay hidden."

Dan asked a question that had bothered him for the last twenty-four hours. "What was Sophie doing up here the day your dad died? Did she have a meeting with Gabriela, or with somebody else?"

Peter looked at him in surprise. "I have no idea. She was up here that day? I don't know… We aren't exactly close… and she probably wouldn't have told me if I asked her. Did you ask her?"

Dan shook his head. "I've never even met her." That was one that he would have to ask Cal about.

Peter Himmel shrugged. "It wasn't to see Dad, I know that. She had no use for him. Maybe it was to bring her daughter up here. Leila."

"Leila is her daughter?" Parker asked.

Peter nodded. "Sophie's love child. And it really bugged her that her daughter got along so well with grandpa."

"How old is Leila?" Dan asked.

"I don't know... ten, eleven, something like that," Peter replied. "About six boyfriends ago, if you know what I mean."

Dan figured it was time to get back on the trail, or they'd never get to Monument Lake.

# chapter 38

The spot where Max Himmel had met his death was still in the shade of the towering granite cliff of the Monument. The massive wall cast a dark shadow over the eastern part of the lake. The huge boulders were cool from the night before, and the men assembled there were shivering after their sweaty climb up from the trailhead. The camping site on the other side of the lake looked warm and inviting in comparison, and Dan couldn't help spending a minute trying to find the spot where he and Kristen had stopped that evening for their conversation. It wasn't easy to find, but he thought he recognized it.

Once they had all arrived, Dan set about organizing the team and explaining what they had done so far. He noticed that the blood from Max's head had seeped into the dirt of the trail, but that some animal had been digging there. In a few days there would be no trace at all. He showed them where he had found the glasses and hearing aid, and three of the agents began a more thorough search of the area.

"We've all walked through this a bunch of times," Peter complained to them, "so I'm not sure what you'll find will be helpful."

One of the older agents, having finally caught his breath after the hike, answered him. "We won't know that until we look, and until we find something. We're used to that."

Parker looked at Peter and said, "This isn't the best situation, but we're used to that. That's why they call us. We'll find something."

Peter didn't seem convinced as he stared out over the lake. Then he turned and looked up at the granite face of the Monument.

"Peter, why don't you stay here and help these guys," Dan said. "You know the area, and maybe that will help. I'll take the rest of the team over to the lake and search that area."

Peter nodded to Dan, then turned back to look up at the cliff. It seemed to Dan that Peter wasn't going to be much help, but Dan was happy to leave the climber in the care of the other search team.

One of the agents had begun to search around the huge boulders, and called out, "Hey, what's this?"

"What you have?" one of the other agents responded.

"It's a bunch of white powder on the ground here," was the response.

Peter Himmel walked quickly over to see. "That's probably chalk—we use it for climbing."

The FBI agent looked long and hard at Peter Himmel.

"Yeah, I used it," said Peter Himmel. "I always use it. And whoever killed my dad used it too—probably to make it look like I was involved." He met the agent's stare.

"It was all over the rock that killed the victim," Dan explained. "But at the time of death, Peter was about five hundred feet up that cliff."

The agent nodded and went back to work, collecting the powder into a bag.

Dan knew that they also needed to search the area where Rafael had been killed, and he decided to lead three of the agents there. Cal had done a good job of describing what he had found there, but Dan wanted to see it for himself.

He followed the trail out of the boulders, and along the east side of Monument Lake, with three of the agents, including Parker, hiking behind him. Here was where he and Cal had first seen Rafael Himmel as he walked along the trail.

Cal said that he had found Rafael's fly rod near where the inlet came into the lake, and Dan peered through the dense growth of alders to see where that might be. As he found a small game trail through the bushes, he pushed through the tangle of limbs and leaves and struggled to find where the stream met the lake.

He could hear the moving water ahead, and managed to find a way through to the edge of the stream. Sure enough, just a few feet away was the large flat slab that Cal had mentioned, sticking well out into the water, and providing a perfect spot for a fisherman. Dan could see why Rafael had stood here. The rock gave him space away from and slightly above the alders, so that he could cast not only into the lake, but also across the stream, and to the fish in the lake that were waiting for anything the stream washed down from above.

Dan turned to see Agent Parker pushing through the alders to join him. The sun was just reaching the outer part of the rock now, and both men crowded out to the very edge so that they could enjoy the sunlight.

"Do you want to get wet?" Dan asked.

Parker looked at him. "What do you mean?"

"Are your sunglasses polarized?" Dan asked him.

Parker shook his head. "I don't know... I don't think so."

Dan took his own sunglasses off and handed them to the FBI agent. "Take a look into the water down there," he said.

Parker removed his glasses and put on Dan's. "Hemostats?" he asked, looking at Dan.

"Medical pliers. Fly fishermen use them to take the hooks out of the fish," Dan explained.

"Okay…" Parker stared into the water. "So it looks like we're going to get wet." Parker turned around to the other two agents, both further back on the rock. "Let's go, guys. We're going wading."

Dan pointed out to the island, maybe fifty yards away. "Cal Healey said he found the fly rod here, and he first saw the body out there," he said. "My guess is that the current carried it out there. It might be worth seeing if that happens—if you can find a piece of wood or something that would float for a while."

Dan's eyes followed the shore of the lake back towards the rocks where Max Himmel's body had been found. The whole area was hidden by the alders, and all he could see was the face of the Monument above them.

"How much does the lake level vary here?" he heard one of the agents ask.

Dan turned around. "It'll go up and down by quite a few feet; much higher during the spring runoff. Even at this time of year, the snow-melt will increase during the day, so the lake might go up a few inches in the afternoon, then back down by early morning.

"So there wouldn't be any reason that this branch over here should be really wet?" the agent asked.

Dan looked at a juniper branch that was lying in the branches of an alder near the agent. He could see that the branch was still waterlogged but lay well above the level of the lake.

"Not unless somebody put it there," he said.

# chapter 39

Dan walked slowly back out to the trail, forcing himself one more time through the dense thicket of alders. Each time he somehow expected them to be easier, and each time he was disappointed. The flexible thin branches seemed to spring back into place, ready to thwart his progress endlessly.

Once out on the trail, Dan imagined himself as a fisherman, approaching the area for the first time. What would Rafael have seen and done? Where would he have gone? As he had watched Rafael fish, Dan remembered that Rafael was standing above the fish and casting downstream, letting the fly drift down with the current. He headed upstream to look for a likely place to start fishing. Rafael would have started upstream and worked his way down with that technique.

The alders around the stream thinned out above the entrance to the lake, and through them Dan could catch glimpses of the moving water. He could see it was a series of shallow riffles over cobblestones, and Dan knew that fly fishermen often preferred the deeper pools where more fish could lie.

The trail climbed slightly uphill, and Dan could hear an increase in the tempo of the water ahead. Through the trees he could see that the trail climbed uphill more steeply, and off to the left, he could see some larger granite slabs. The stream would have to cross them somewhere.

A faint use trail broke off to the left, and Dan followed it out of the trees and onto the warm, cream-colored granite. The sun was bright here, and Dan's shadow stood out starkly against the pale granite.

A deep rift in the granite showed him where the stream had gone. As he approached the edge, he could hear roaring water below, and was not surprised to see a cascade of white water sluicing through the narrow cut in the granite. This water was too fast to fish, and Dan looked upstream, where a wide shallow pool was dammed by the granite slabs. A small fish spooked and raced upstream when Dan's silhouette came into view, but the pool was too shallow, and the bottom too uniform to hold many fish.

Dan's feet fell lightly on the granite as he walked back down to see what the stream held below the cascade. As he peered over the edge of the rock, he could see a cloud of whitewater leading into a deep pool. For thousands, perhaps tens of thousands of years, the stream had followed this same course. And as it did so, it had slowly worn down the softer rock beneath the granite slabs. How deep was the pool? The color of the water, even in bright daylight, was a deep blue-black, and Dan could not see the bottom. Fifteen feet? Twenty? Deep enough to hide a cloud of trout.

Dan looked around to see where Rafael might have stood to fish the pool. Where he stood now was no good. Any fish hooked in the pool would have to be dragged up through the cascade of whitewater, and that same powerful current would have made the drift of the fly unmanageable.

A slight breeze drifted upstream from the lake, so Rafael would have wanted to stay on this side of the stream. But the granite on this side of the stream continued in a series of pillowy hummocks down the side of the pool, and thirty feet further down, Dan could see a way to get closer to the water, and to the fish.

He stepped back away from the stream and walked down to the lower section, keeping his form hidden from the fish. As he crept back up to the stream over the mounded granite, he could see another faint trail, where many fishermen before him had solved this same puzzle. Dan followed the trail down to the pool and found it led to a spot next to a large fir on a ledge about six feet above the water.

Here his feet found just a small patch of dirt, and Dan could see the footprints of someone who had been here recently, since the rains last week. Rafael would have stood here, with the tree on his left, and flicked the fly into the headwaters of the pool, letting it drift.

Dan counted four fish still in the pool, and who knew how many more lurked in the deeper part, where they could not be seen.

Rafael Himmel would have fished here for a while. After he had caught a few of the fish, the rest would have been spooked, and Rafael would find them less willing to attack the fly. Or maybe he spooked them by being too aggressive or casting badly. Dan waved his arm over his head, and two of the fish slowly drifted down into the depths of the pool. It wouldn't have taken much to scare the others. Dan wondered how many fish Rafael had taken from this pool.

As he turned away from the stream, Dan looked at the tree next to him. From one of the branches hanging out over the stream, Dan could see the glitter of a small thread of monofilament: the remains of a fly fisherman's leader, snagged in the tree. There would be a fly at the end of it, too high in the tree to be salvaged. Was it Rafael's?

Dan walked back out onto the warm granite slabs next to the creek. The sound of the rushing water covered up all the other noises of the wilderness, and Dan realized how easy it was to feel completely alone here.

He looked down the stream for the next fishing spot and saw a series of boulders sticking out of the water. He was sure that one of them, down near the very end of the stretch of stream that was visible from his position, was where he and Cal had talked to Rafael the first day. So he hadn't traveled far. And what he had seen that day had to be visible from somewhere nearby.

The sun was warm enough that Dan stepped into the shade of a large pine that grew on the edge of the granite. From here he could not see the face of the Monument; that was too far around to the left. Alders covered much of the side of the stream, and between them the open forest gave way to the talus and scree that were part of the side of the granite massif of the Monument.

The breeze from the lake stalled, and to his surprise, Dan felt a waft of cold air brush into him. His head turned again to the left, to try and see through the trees. He walked along the granite slabs, looking up towards the rocks that formed the side of the Monument. He could see what looked like a game trail leading up through the manzanita there, and yes, behind that tree.

He could see now that there was a narrow chute of rocks and debris, now overgrown with Mountain Misery brush, that led upwards out of the canyon. It was no more than fifty yards away. The cool air was washing down that chute towards him. Was this what Rafael had seen? Is this where the mysterious man in camouflage had been? Dan struck out with long strides to cover the ground towards the chute.

As he neared the chute, Dan thought about the others. Should he call them? It seemed unnecessary. They were busy in areas that were clearly important, and this might well be a wild goose chase. If he found something that really mattered, there would be plenty of time to call.

The base of the chute was complicated by a large fallen log, and for a moment Dan considered stopping right there. But he could see, just past the log, that there was a way to get up over the first big rocks, and possibly around to the left, beyond that.

There was no pretty way around the log. It was too large to step over, and it lay two feet off the ground: too low to go under. Dan forgot about his dignity and leaned over the log, kicking first one foot and then the other up on top of it, then allowing himself to slide down the other side. Just before his feet hit the ground, he got a glimpse of the dirt where they were going to land. And in that dirt there were footprints. Not the waffle-soled boots of Rafael Himmel.

These had been made by someone else.

# chapter 40

Dan pushed through the bushes around the log and found the first trace of a track that went left around a large boulder. From there he could see a way to get further up the chute. The rock here was new and clean, with sharp corners from where it had broken off from the fractures above.

The first few of these rocks served as a kind of oversized stairway, and Dan stepped up them, one after the other, climbing quickly up the chute. At the top he found a steep granite ramp that led him further up the slope, to what looked like the path of a seasonal stream that drained the chute.

It wasn't complicated to follow the ramp, but Dan realized that he was going up fast. The beating in his chest and the gasps for breath told him that this was far steeper than the trail up to the lake.

The top of the granite ramp faded into a small flat of gravel, where the stream paused briefly before plunging down the chute. Dan could see that for the next few yards he would have to pick his way through smaller rocks and some debris that the stream had carried down from above. He took three or four big steps uphill and then stopped, catching his breath from the exertion. As he turned around to look below, he could see that he was already climbing above some of the smaller trees on the valley floor, and the view was beginning to open up towards the top of the valley. He turned and continued up the chute.

Progress was slow, but at every step Dan could see that the chute continued upwards. While he didn't have to think about where he was going, he did have to place each foot carefully. Some of the rocks were not stable, and one or two rocked under his weight. At one point, on a section of muddy dirt and scree at the center of the chute, Dan's foot slid backwards through the mud, and he made a mental note to try and put his foot on rock wherever possible. At another point, further up the slope, he could see where another hiker had also slipped, leaving a deep, wet gash in the slope.

It was hard work. Dan tried to find a pace that would allow him to move steadily upwards, but each step was a new adventure, and that worked against him. He paused every eight to ten steps to breathe, and he could feel the cold sweat on his shirt when he did. It may have been warm out in the sun, but here in the narrow chute, the temperature was at least ten degrees colder. Dan would not have been surprised to find small traces of snow deep in the shaded crevices above him.

Two hundred feet up the chute, Dan came to a large boulder that seemed to block further progress. Wedged between the two sheer granite walls, the boulder hung above him ominously. He stopped and put a hand on the boulder, resting.

Behind him the valley to the east was in glorious sunlight, and Dan could see the bare peaks of the Sierra crest at the top of the valley. Across the valley walls of granite were interspersed with thin forests on the slopes, and he could just hear the rush of the water in the creek if he listened above his labored breathing.

But the steep walls of the chute blocked him from seeing Monument Lake and anything to the west. His feet, perched precariously on the rubble below the boulder, began to ache from the effort of keeping him in place. He shifted his feet and took a position on the left-hand side of the chute. From here he could see a series of small ledges in the wall of the chute, leading up and beyond the boulder. They looked as if he might be able to climb them, but Dan remembered well his early lessons in rock climbing: you don't climb up anything without knowing how you are going to get back down.

Dan tested the first ledge and stepped up on it. Above, there were solid handholds, and Dan felt comfortable in moving to the second ledge. The moves came easily to him, and he took pleasure in seeing his body respond to the challenge of the rock.

He was now three or four feet above the floor of the chute, his back now very close to the mass of the hanging boulder. But the ledges on the eastern wall were running out. They were getting thinner, and Dan didn't trust them anymore. As he leaned back to look up, Dan saw that it would be easy to transfer his weight over to the side of the boulder itself. There was an easy foothold there that was hidden from below. And with three more moves, Dan was above the boulder, and now climbing up the chute again on foot.

Where would it lead? Dan hoped that it would give him a view over Monument Lake, and all that lay below. Perhaps from up here, Dan could get a better sense of what had happened there over the past three days. At the very least, he hoped to be able to see the search teams, and possibly direct them from above.

The upper section of the chute was easier now, and Dan made excellent progress. It was still steep, and his breath still came in gasps, but the footwork no longer took much thought, and rocks seemed more stable here. He could see above him, and saw that in another fifty feet or so, it looked like the sun would find its way down into the chute. Dan realized that this mean the chute was gradually altering its direction.

As he climbed, the steep chute became slightly shallower, and Dan could almost see over the edge to the west. His right hand was now in sunshine, and he stopped for a moment to catch his breath and look around again.

On the far side of the valley, the ridge top was no longer high above him. In fact, he could see that his own position must be well more than a few hundred feet above the valley floor. Above him, the rocks blocked his view. The chute was now almost completely rock, as any debris had washed down far below. Dan looked back down the chute and could still see the big boulder that had blocked his way. Below that, he could see the tops of trees on the valley floor, looking more like toys than towering pines.

Dan turned back and continued up the chute. Now it was clearly Class 3, some of the scrambling required his hands, and Dan knew that a slip would cause serious injury. He carefully pulled himself over a ledge and found himself at the top of the chute. It ended abruptly on a small ledge, with huge fingers of granite looming above it. Without climbing gear there was certainly no way for Dan to continue upwards.

This was bare rock now, and Dan sat down on the ledge at the top of the chute and looked around. He could see one of the members of the search team by the lake was still in the water, and another was on the rock slab in the lake. He assumed the others would be somewhere in the alders.

It was harder to see the team in the boulders below. A narrow crest of rock blocked his view of the foot of the Monument, and Dan could not see the boulders at all. But across the lake he could see the campsite. It looked as if Cal or some of his team might have reached that. Dan checked his watch and was surprised; it had taken him only a few minutes to climb the chute, and that meant that Cal's team had spent little time down on the trail before moving up to the campsite by the lake. He wondered why.

And there, along the shore, was where he had chatted with Kristen.

# chapter 41

Dan pulled out his water bottle and took a swallow. His breathing was returning to normal now and he allowed himself to feel a small tinge of satisfaction. He was in pretty good shape these days, and his recovery time was nice and short. Within a few minutes, he would feel perfectly rested.

His mind went drifting back to the day he was sitting down next to the body of Max Himmel. And as he did that day, his eyes scanned the area around the top of the chute for anything he might see.

Just next to his left leg was a small smudge of dried mud, right on the edge of the ledge. Whoever came up here before him had made it this far. But then what?

Dan craned his neck around to see the rocks above him. They were just too steep for him to consider climbing. Dan was willing to debate the topic internally, but the more he looked at the smooth, nearly vertical rock, the more he was convinced that he should not try to climb it.

If it had been in a gym, with a safe belay, he would have tried without a second thought. But up here, if he fell, the result was sure to be serious injury or death. He stood up to check one more time, and was convinced. It was not the day for folly.

He looked back down the chute and was amazed at how steep and forbidding it looked, even from above. It is always easier to climb up something than to climb down it, and Dan realized that his trip down was going to take a certain amount of courage and care—not something he looked forward to, but he was sure that he could do it.

A hummingbird buzzed into view, attracted, perhaps, by the patch on Dan's hat. It zipped up in front of him, and just as quickly decided that Dan was not, in fact, a flower. The bird hovered off the cliff face to the west of Dan before shooting off into space.

Dan's gaze wandered from the hummingbird to the face of granite to the west of him. Was that a reasonable foothold below him? The granite billowed out a few inches from the rock face about six feet below Dan, and it looked as if that lip then continued around onto the face of the Monument.

How high was he? Dan wondered where he was in relationship to the famous ledge that Peter had reached. He couldn't tell from where he was, but if he could see just a bit further around the corner, the ledge would certainly come into view, wouldn't it?

Dan's heart began to race as he considered his options. How could he get down to the lip of granite? He would have to turn around, and slowly ease his body down the face. He peered over the edge again, and his stomach turned icy. If he missed the lip, he would slip, slide and fall hundreds of feet down, probably smacking into the jagged rocks he could see far below.

He sat back and thought about it. There was no need to do this, he assured himself. He leaned over and looked again. There was a small juniper wedged on the edge of the chute below him. Could he go back there, then try to ease his way out onto the lip of granite? It seemed worth exploring.

He took his time getting down to the little tree. It was only six feet, but he wanted to give himself time to think this over, and make sure that he wasn't doing anything stupid. When he was standing with his feet next to the tiny juniper, he checked again. No sudden moves, he reminded himself. Take it easy and slow. Let's just see what happens. But no silly risks.

He eased his right foot over the juniper and felt along with his boot. Yes, the lip of granite was there and seemed large enough for comfort. He reached out with his right hand and felt a small nub of granite: enough to keep him centered over his feet. Slowly, he eased his weight over onto his right foot. Everything seemed quite solid. He moved his left hand onto the face as well, and with that established, he lifted his left foot over the juniper and out onto the lip.

He was now fully on the face of the Monument, but he still couldn't see much, as the granite wall curved around to his right out of sight. He was tempted to go back, to retrace his movements back to the chute just for practice, but realized that all this had been quite easy. If he just kept calm, and focused, he didn't need to worry.

His right foot edged forward again, still finding solid footing. And his right hand found another small anchor. Left hand and foot followed. He still couldn't see the ledge, but he could see that the granite lip went further around the face. It got a bit thinner as it went along, but it was still there.

For the next few minutes, Dan slowly eased himself out onto the face of the Monument. None of the moves were technically difficult, and the thin lip of granite was still there, although now it wasn't wide enough for more than a quarter of the width of his boot. He leaned tightly into the wall to make sure that his hand did not have to overcome much weight, keeping everything directly over his feet. But the concentration was taking its toll. Dan was sweating profusely, and he knew it wasn't because of the workload—it was the stress of hanging his body on a tiny lip of granite five hundred feet high.

The far face of the Monument was now in view, and only a small center section was still hidden behind a curve in the face. Dan realized that the ledge must be in that center section. He stopped for a minute, to calm his nerves and try to let his muscles relax. It wasn't easy.

His breath was calmer now, and Dan pressed his face to the granite and closed his eyes. It was time to go back. There was no point in going further out onto the face of the cliff, and he could feel his energy flagging. It was better to go back now, before this got dangerous.

As he stood there, clinging to the granite face of the Monument, he was surprised to hear noises from quite nearby. He heard a zipper run, and nylon rustling. Somebody else was on the cliff with him, and not far away.

Dan thought about this for a moment. He knew the department had not allowed anyone in the area because of the search operation. Who was up here? Not someone with the search party. This had to be someone else.

Dan slowly edged out on the lip a few more feet. His right hand found only smooth granite, and he held on tightly with his left hand. He reached out further with his right hand and felt nothing but smooth granite.

A flicker of motion, a brief shadow above him, caught his eye and he strained his neck to look up, while still keeping his body as close as possible to the face of the cliff. He could feel the sole of his shoe slowly bending under his weight and wondered how long he could count on that. Dan didn't dare look down now, and he knew he couldn't hold this position for long.

Again, the shadow of motion flickered above him. Dan strained, and suddenly saw a head and shoulders lean out over him. Peter Himmel's face appeared only fifteen or twenty feet above him on the cliff. The surprise on Peter's face quickly turned to dismay.

Dan noted the camouflage shirt that Peter was wearing. Of course. If Peter knew about the chute, then the climbing expert would have been able to get up and down the cliff in minutes. It dissolved the timing of Peter's alibi into thin air.

# chapter 42

"I don't think you can get up here from there," Peter Himmel called out to him. "At least, I don't think you can!" The stress made it clear that Peter could have done so.

Sweat dripped down into Dan's eyes as he baked in the heat from the granite wall. But he couldn't spare a hand to wipe it away. He leaned in to the wall, to take some of the strain off his left hand and answered Peter. "So how did you do it?"

"When you get to the top of the Backstairs, you have to go up first, then traverse and drop down from above," Peter responded. "I guess you missed that part."

Dan realized that his hands were sweating, too. That wouldn't help the grip that he had on the granite wall. "Yeah, I guess I did," Dan replied. He leaned in to the wall and rested. The sun was directly in his eyes as he looked up, and he could feel a hint of panic rise in his chest. He was still trying to figure out how Peter had been seen on the ledge while he must have been climbing up and down the chute.

Dan took a deep breath. His heart was beating very fast, and he tried to slow it down so that he could think this through. He tried to find the little nub of granite that had seemed like such a strong anchor for his right hand, but it didn't seem to be where he thought it was. He really needed to take some weight off his right foot, which was slowly beginning to slip off the lip of granite.   He knew he had to be very careful right now.

Peter's voice called out to him from above. "You weren't supposed to find that staircase. That makes things a lot more complicated."

"Is that what Rafael did?" Dan asked.

Peter paused before answering. "He didn't get the whole picture. With Dad out of the way, we could each do what we wanted. That's all. But he wouldn't let it go. He thought he could force me to do what he wanted. And he's not that smart."

Dan wanted to reach for the radio, to call down to the team below, but he couldn't reach the radio with his right hand, and his left hand was clinging to the best handhold he had. His left leg began to tremble slightly, and Dan knew that it was only a matter of time before that got worse. Again he tried to focus his breathing and calm down.

Dan felt a smack on his left shoulder and tried to look up at Peter.

He really should have called for backup from the top of the chute. But at that point, he'd had no idea that Peter was up here. He could hear Peter moving things around up on the ledge. He considered screaming for help, but the rest were so far below, they would never be able to help.

"I have quite a few rocks up here," Peter stated calmly. "Sorry, but you weren't supposed to figure this out."

Dan turned his head to the left, to see how far he would have to go to get back to the chute. He couldn't take the weight off his left foot, because his right foot still felt unstable. But somehow, he had to get back to the chute. He could see just the very tip of the juniper branch sticking out into air off the cliff, seeming to reach out to him. The sharp tips of the needles seemed to float in the air.

The inflatable doll. The thought hit Dan hard. Peter had dressed the doll up in his climbing clothes and posed it on the ledge. That's how Luke and Veronica had seen someone up on the ledge, dressed in Peter's red climbing shirt.

He called to Peter Himmel. "If I fall, don't you think the guys down there will come up and find you?"

"I don't think they can," replied Peter. "And I can be up over the top of this thing and into the backcountry before they have time to do anything about it."

Dan thought this over. He turned his head back to the right, where it was easier to see the motions above. "Where do you think you can hide?" he asked. "That might work for a few days or weeks, but you can't stay hidden forever. And you know as well as I do that you can't live off the land up here."

"Oh, I won't be living off the land up here," Peter answered. "I just need a little head start, and I can lose these guys forever."

Another rock smacked down on Dan, this one hitting the side of his head, and then crashing into his back. The blow stunned Dan momentarily, and it took a minute for him to realize through the pain that he was now bleeding. The sweat on his head burned even more as it ran into the cut. His right foot was now somewhat numb, and Dan had no idea how much longer it would stay on the tiny lip of granite.

With his right hand, Dan fastened onto a small handhold. It did not seem nearly so solid a grip as the one he had earlier, but he was determined to hang on. It was the best he could do. He looked down at his feet, but he was so close to the wall that he could see very little. The white brilliance of the granite below blurred his vision, already struggling through the sweat in his eyes. The heat from the rock was radiating like a stove.

The next rock hit Dan squarely on the left hand, and after the initial numb shock he knew that the hand had been hurt. He couldn't feel some of his fingers, and he had no idea if they could continue to keep him close to the rock. The ache of his muscles was becoming unbearable, and he knew he had to do something quickly.

Dan heard another noise, a kind of smack against the granite above him and a boom sounded from behind him somewhere. At first Dan thought it was a sonic boom from an airplane, but it was too sharp for that. He tried to look up.

Peter was perched hanging over the ledge, looking down the cliff, but his eyes were not on Dan. They were focused further down the cliff.

Another smack, followed by another boom. This time there was a grunt from Peter: "Shit."

From below, Dan could hear voices yelling. He could not make out what they were saying. It occurred to him that the officers below were shooting. He tried to look down but simply couldn't see. Above him the shadow moved again, and Dan braced himself for another rock.

But this time the motion was different. Dan tried to look up through the sweat and hair that were plastered to his face. Peter was standing on the edge of the ledge, his right hand over his head. Dan could see that Peter's left arm was dangling at his side, and a dark splotch stained his shirtsleeve.

In the back of his mind, Dan was vaguely aware of the noise of a helicopter in the background.

He couldn't bear it any longer. Dan moved, not with grace and thought, but out of sheer panic. His right and left hands clutched desperately at the rock, and he placed as much weight as he dared on his right foot. For just an instant, it held, and he nudged his left foot further back along the narrow rock lip.

And then his right foot slipped. The jolt of that jerked his right hand free, and for a moment Dan hung on the cliff with only his injured left hand and his left foot. His stomach tensed into a painful knot of cramps, and he jerked his right foot back into place along the lip. His right hand waved frantically across the face of the rock and found another little nub to catch onto.

Dan heard Peter Himmel swear very quietly above him. Dan looked up and could see Peter was now staring at Dan with a strange look in his eyes. "Keep your weight on your feet, and use your hands for control," Peter said to Dan. But his eyes seemed out of focus, distant.

"I'm trying," Dan yelled, not at all confident that he could continue to do so. He wondered about the change in Peter's personality.

"This really sucks," said Peter. Then he gave a groan.

Dan looked up. Peter was pale, and tottering above him. His eyes caught Dan's briefly. "Good luck," he whispered.

In the next instant, Dan saw Peter tumble forward into the air above him, sailing far out beyond the face of the cliff, and plummeting below.

# chapter 43

Dan could hear the sound of the helicopter somewhere behind him, but he couldn't turn around to see where it was. Not that it would have mattered. With his eyes blinded by sweat, he couldn't see much at all, only large shapes.

The throbbing pain in his head continued, but he was more worried about the pain in his left hand. It was no longer even a little bit numb, and it hurt every time that he tried to put any weight on it. His two middle fingers seemed to hurt the most, and Dan found himself trying to hold onto the rock with just his thumb and forefinger. Faintly, in the back of his mind, he could hear himself thinking, "So this is how it ends. How odd."

He shifted his left foot another six inches back towards the chute and found good footing there again. This time, when he moved his right foot back, he tried to turn it around so it was facing the same way. That gave him a bit more stability.

His left hand slowly reached for something that he could hold. What there was gave him little confidence, but he didn't have any other option. He focused hard on where his left hand had been and tried to quickly shift his right hand onto that same hold. It was there.

He took a deep breath, but it didn't help. He was still panting.

From behind him, the chopper was now louder, and Dan heard a loud-speaker roar to life. "Do you want us to attempt a rescue?" The chopper hovered behind him.

Dan couldn't think about that. He could only think about hanging on, about making sure that he didn't get distracted from his two hands and his two feet. He tried to shake his head, but he wasn't sure that the chopper could even tell that he had done it.

"Do you want us to attempt a rescue?" the loudspeaker roared again.

Dan kept his right hand tightly on the rock and balanced on his feet. With his left hand he slowly moved his fingers together and pointed at his neck, then waved his hand back and forth in front of his neck. With equal care, he slowly moved the hand back onto the rock.

Dan heard the noise of the chopper slowly drift away, and then soar up and away above him. He took another deep breath and slowly moved his left foot forward again. He remembered that at some point the narrow shelf had broken off for a few inches. It hadn't seemed important on the way out, when he could see clearly what he was doing, and was full of confidence. Now he remembered, and each step became an exploration, searching for that missing lip.

It was only about thirty-five feet that he had to cover, but it felt like it took him hours. At one point after having found the missing lip and carefully easing himself over it, Dan realized that this was not a difficult physical maneuver he was executing. Once over that obstacle, he knew that his body was capable of getting him off the granite face of the cliff. But he also knew that more climbers died on the way down than on the way up; that he needed to fight the feeling of relief that was flooding his veins.

He pushed on without seeing, not really knowing how far he had come, or how far he had to go. First left foot, very gently, then right foot, sliding over. His face was pressed to the rock. His left hand was really weak now, but the lip was wider, and that helped. Then his right hand was becoming the key piece of the puzzle, moving quickly from one hold to the next, not leaving him without some kind of pull towards the face.

He was exhausted. He leaned into the rock, allowing his body to rest for a moment. He could feel a breeze on his face, drying the sweat off his back. It felt cool, and Dan wished that it would dry the sweat of his face so he could see.

Left foot—and now something was pushing against him. Dan panicked for a second and began to try and shake his leg free. It would not let go, and then he realized it was the juniper. He was back at the chute. He opened his eyes as wide as he could and yes, there was the tiny tree, clinging to its home in the crack in the rock.

"Up and over, slow but sure," he told himself. His legs began to shake, and he made two moves, rolled over the edge, and fell down into the little ledge at the top of the chute. His breath came in gasps, but Dan was able to pull out his handkerchief and wipe the sweat out of his eyes. His breath would not slow down, but only came in bigger gasps, gasps he could not control, and he started sobbing with relief.

He reached down for his radio and called to report his position. The team below assured him that he should stay where he was. They would take care of him from here. Dan leaned back and pulled out his water bottle. As he tried to take the top off with his left hand, the cap slipped from his fingers, and he watched it bounce down the chute, rattling and smacking for what seemed like many seconds.

He stared after it, then lay back and waited for the rescue team.

# chapter 44

·

The rest of the afternoon was always going to be blurry in Dan's memory. As he lay with his eyes closed, he felt something on his arm. At first, he thought it was a snake. It moved again and Dan slowly opened his eyes as if the rest of his body was frozen in place. It moved again, a long thin red line, and Dan realized it was a climbing rope. The rope began wiggle and dance, and within a minute Dan looked up at Bob Tschida in full mountain rescue outfit, rappelling down into the chute.

Bob quickly asked Dan how he felt and inspected his head and hand. Dan had the very strange sensation that Bob was not so much worried about his injured hand and head, as much as he worried about his mental condition. As if to prove him right, Dan suggested that they start down the chute as soon as Bob was ready.

Bob took one look down the rock-filled channel and turned back to Dan. "I don't think so," he said. "I think we're going to get choppered out of here."

Dan said that he thought that was unnecessary.

Bob smiled and said, "Not your decision. It's mine," and proceeded to put Dan in the harness and safety lines. A few minutes later Dan watched the cable slowly swing down from above. Bob corralled the cable, clipped in, and then Dan was hoisted, wrapped around Bob

Tschida like an ardent lover, up into the air and reeled into the chopper.

Dan stopped thinking. He was now just a passenger. Bob handed him some water and an energy bar, and Dan took them without a word. Within minutes they were landing at the hospital.

A full reception committee was there to meet them, and Dan was put immediately into a wheelchair and rolled into the ER. The doors swung closed behind him, and he went from one nurse to the next: washing his head, taking X-rays of his hand, lying face down on a gurney, sewing the cut in his scalp, wrapping his hand in a bandage that seemed far too large and white than was needed.

Dan was beyond making conversation, and he just watched as one white-coated person after the next came into his room, or rolled him into another room, did something to him, or asked him for more information.

Two fingers on his left hand were broken, but they would not need surgery. They put fourteen stitches in the back of his head, and the bandages were truly impressive.

Then he was back in a wheelchair and rolling out to the front of the hospital, where Cal Healey was waiting.

"I thought you might need a ride," Cal said with a grin.

Dan's mind was still a little cloudy. Had they given him something for pain in the hospital? "Yeah, thanks, that would be great," he said to Cal.

Cal helped him into the squad car and got behind the wheel. "That was some pretty fancy climbing up there," he said to Dan.

Dan put his hand over his face and muttered, "Don't ever let me do that again."

Cal chuckled. "Hell, you didn't ask my opinion this time!"

Dan rested his head back on the headrest and closed his eyes.

When he opened his eyes, he saw that they were on their way past Columbia, not towards Dan's house.

"Hey, where are we going?" he asked Cal.

"You're having dinner at my house," Cal answered. "Maggie insisted. Because you don't have anything to eat at your place, and you can't cook anyway."

Dan couldn't bring himself to argue.

At the house, Cal sat Dan down on the sofa and suggested that he lie down if he wanted to. The suggestion made sense to Dan, and he only woke up when Cal's eleven-year-old daughter Lisa came into the house, yelling.

Amid much shushing from her parents, Lisa stopped and stared at Dan on the sofa.

"Hi, Lisa," Dan said quietly to her, and smiled.

"Hi..." Lisa responded carefully. "What happened to you?"

Dan thought this over. "I had a little climbing accident," he finally answered.

Cal called out from the kitchen. "He was chasing a bad guy up a cliff."

Lisa's eyes got wide. "Did you catch him?"

"No," Dan admitted.

"Yes," Cal called out from the other room.

Maggie called everyone to the table.

After dinner, Cal drove Dan to his house. They drove in silence for a few minutes, and then Dan asked, "Is Peter dead?"

"Oh yeah," Cal replied. "And just so you know, he fell way off to the side from where his father died. There's no way a rock from where

Peter was up on the ledge could have fallen to hit his father. Did he say anything to you up there?"

"Not really. Rafael tried to blackmail him. Just before he jumped, he wished me good luck," Dan said.

"That's quite a family," Cal noted again, shaking his head. "I guess they had some pretty bad arguments up there. Max was pretty tough on them. Peter didn't take that so well."

"I guess not," Dan agreed. "You know, I think all Peter really wanted to do was to live and climb in the mountains. He just couldn't stand the idea of spending the rest of his life working in an office. That was torture for him." The lights on the dashboard seemed oddly comforting to him. "Did you find anything on the trail about the shooter?"

Cal snorted. "I found one of Kristen Gallagher's potato peelers about ten feet from the tree that Peter was standing behind. That and a small paper bag. I'm guessing that he cut himself just to confuse us. The bag was just for sound effects."

"Well," Dan nodded, "that worked."

"For a while," Cal admitted. "How did you figure this out?"

"I didn't," Dan said. "I just wanted to see what Rafael might have seen—that guy in camo that nobody else saw."

"And you did," Cal pointed out.

"Yeah…" Dan agreed. "I guess I did."

Cal pulled the car up in front of Dan's house and helped Dan up to the porch. "Do you need anything?" he asked the ranger.

"No, I'm fine. Thanks, Cal. And thank Maggie again for dinner," Dan answered.

Cal held his hand out. "You know, what you did up there was real…. well, it was real courage," Cal said.

Dan gave a rueful laugh. "Yeah... I don't want to do that again."

And he turned and walked inside.

# chapter 45

The house was dark and Dan didn't feel much like turning on any lights. He heard Cal start his car and drive away. Dan sat down in the chair at his desk. He really wanted to shower, but wasn't sure quite how he was going to do that with his bandages.

Out of habit, he reached down and turned on his computer, carefully using the index finger of his right hand. As it booted up, he checked the phone. There were no messages.

The computer screen flickered to life and lit the house with its dim cool blue glow.

Dan picked up the phone. There was something he had been wanting to do for a while now. He laid his phone on the desk and slowly began to punch in Kristen Gallagher's phone number.

After the first few numbers, he stopped, full of doubts. If a man answered the phone, what should Dan do? Tell her about the potato peeler?

He dialed the rest of the numbers. It didn't matter now.

The phone rang three, then four times. Dan decided not to leave a message.

And then a voice answered, "Hello?"

Was it Kristen?

"Hello, Kristen Gallagher?" Dan offered.

"Yes, this is Kristen," she replied.

"Hi, Kristen. This is Dan Courtwright."